TO SPOIL THE SUN

TO SPOIL THE SUN

JOYCE ROCKWOOD

HENRY HOLT AND COMPANY

NEW YORK

Published by Henry Holt and Company, Inc.,
521 Fifth Avenue, New York, New York 10175.
Distributed in Canada by Fitzhenry & Whiteside Limited,
195 Allstate Parkway, Markham, Ontario L3R 4T8.

Library of Congress Cataloging in Publication Data
Rockwood, Joyce.
To spoil the sun.
Summary: Forewarned by omens, an Indian
village is struck by an "invisible fire" which actually
is smallpox brought to America by European explorers.
[1. Indians of North America—Fiction] I. Title.
PZ7.R597To   [Fic]   76-10568
ISBN 0-8050-0293-6

Printed in the United States of America
3 5 7 9 10 8 6 4 2

ISBN 0-8050-0293-6

For my grandmother
Palmer Cary Graves
whose baby brother died
of smallpox

TO SPOIL THE SUN

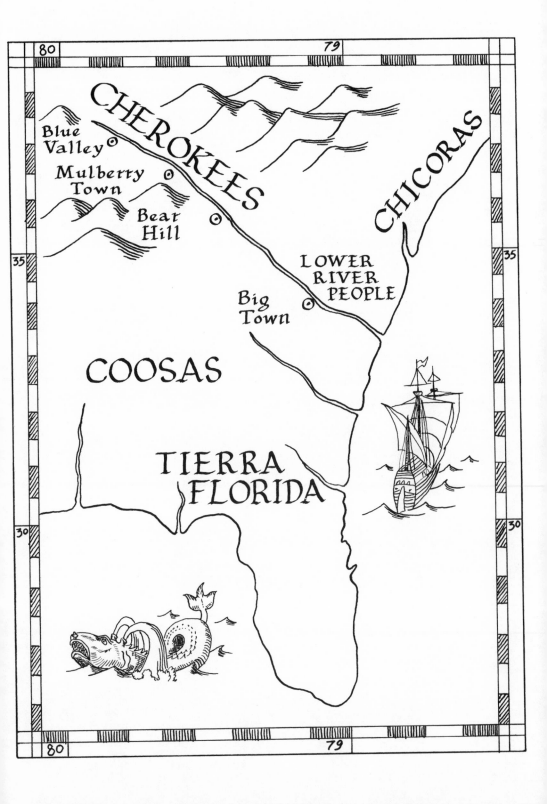

ONE

There were four omens. I was young, only nine years old, when the first omen came. I heard it discussed around the fire, told and retold until it became a part of my own knowledge, until it became as if I had witnessed it myself.

The first omen came to Mink alone. Only he saw the hawk dive into the cornfield. He saw it strike down in the midst of brown stalks and rise with a snake in its talons. A snake in winter in the cornfield. A rattlesnake in the cold of winter. Mink saw the hawk rise, beating its wings, the snake writhing beneath. He watched the hawk as it struggled with its prey, as it beat its wings toward the brown hills beyond the valley. He saw the snake whip suddenly, striking its fangs into the heart of the hawk. The hawk stiffened and fluttered down through the stillness of the air. Mink ran toward them as they fell and he saw them sprawl against the earth. He saw the snake crawl away through the dry weeds beneath the broken stalks. He went after it to see where it would go. But already it had disappeared. He went back to the hawk. As he looked at it, piteously dead upon the earth, he was seized with fear, and he hurried back to Quail Town.

My father was the watchman that day. He stood atop the

palisade, on one of the bastions in the wall of closely set timbers. He saw Mink coming up through the valley. My father knew Mink was disturbed. He knew it by the way his bearskin robe was drawn too tightly about his shoulders. He saw Mink cross the log bridge over the ditch outside the palisade. He saw him wind through the wall's entrance and pass along the streets between the houses to the open plaza in the town's center. There, Mink went directly to Gray Hawk's house, a small dwelling beside the great townhouse.

Inside he sat with Gray Hawk at the fire. After they had smoked together, Mink told him what he had seen. Gray Hawk sent for Shaker and then for several other beloved men. In their age and wisdom they smoked tobacco and talked. Late in the afternoon it was decided that Mink should speak to the Seven Clans in council.

In the evening when the people had gathered in the townhouse, Shaker spoke to them for Gray Hawk, announcing that Mink wished to address the council. They divided then into seven clans, each person moving to his proper seat on the tiers of benches, all the clans in order, forming a circle around the great room. The fire was in the circle's center, Ancient Fire, flickering, throwing its dim light upon the Seven Clans.

The pipes were passed to open the council, to bring the people together into one mind. Then Mink rose to speak.

"People of the Seven Clans! I stand before you as your nephew, and as your brother, and as your uncle. Whenever I speak to you within this circle, standing as I am before this Ancient Fire, it is a walk we take together along the straight path of truth. I see the path now stretched before us. Come and let us walk upon it. Let me speak to you about a certain matter."

Mink told them of the disturbing things he had seen in the cornfield. A snake, traveler of the warm seasons, going about the earth in the cold of winter. And worse, a bird of the sun struck dead from the sky by a creature of the Lower World. Mink's words were like the fangs of the snake striking into the heart of the Seven Clans. Fear swept in a circle around the fire. As Mink took his seat, another of the beloved men rose to speak.

"People of the Seven Clans! You who are my brothers and my sisters; you who are my nieces and my nephews; you who are my grandchildren. The words of my younger brother are straight, but the truth does not always put our hearts at ease. We ask ourselves what it means that he has seen such a thing. Does it mean that our corn will fail? People of the Seven Clans, we must prepare against a famine. I think this is the meaning of what was seen."

Mink rose again. "My older brother is very wise. He has often seen the true shape of strange events. I am not so wise, and perhaps that is why I fear that some misfortune even greater than this has been foretold. But what could it be? I myself do not know."

The incident was discussed throughout the night, Mink repeating the story, adding to it every detail he could remember. Different ones thought they knew what it meant, but in the end there was no consensus. The council adjourned without deciding what to do.

When in the same winter the second omen came, it was for everyone to see. I myself remember it clearly. It began with a thunderstorm that awakened me in the night, a violent storm with beating rain and crashing thunder. I lay frightened in the darkness and heard my mother say to my father, "Thunder in winter. It is not good."

I called out to my mother.

"Go to sleep, my little daughter," she said. "It is nothing. Listen to the rain on the roof and let it take you to sleep again."

I pulled the blanket over my head and listened to the rain striking against the bark roof and to my mother and father whispering together in their bed. Then outside the house there was noise and confusion, there were people running in the streets between the houses. "Seven Clans, come running! The warriors' tree is burning!"

My father leaped from his bed, and my brothers too, and they ran out into the rain, my mother following behind. No one told me to stay or to come. I jumped up and went with them, although I did not understand the reason for the excitement. Women were wailing. People were running through the town and out through the palisade entrance and over the ditch to stand and look across the valley at the warriors' tree. I followed my brothers to a bastion in the palisade and they began scrambling up to the top.

"Let me!" I cried, and Two Crows stopped and helped me up until I was standing beside him at the top, looking out over the valley, staring at the small orange glow in the distance. The rain had turned to a fine drizzle. Beneath us were the people watching the light of the burning tree. A few men were running out across the valley, while others were returning, crying as they ran, "It is the warriors' tree!" Women were wailing; they loosened their hair and let it fall disheveled, as if someone had died. I began to tremble, not because I understood what was happening, but because the women were wailing and because the men were running and shouting.

It was not until later that I knew the reason for their distress. The tree that burned was the honey locust tree. That was where the warriors stopped when they returned victorious from the war trail. They would hang their scalps and other trophies on the long thorns of the tree and paint themselves for celebration while a herald ran to the town to announce their return and their victory. The people would come to the tree to meet the warriors and lead them back to the town in a joyous procession. The honey locust is Thunder's tree, and Thunder is the force that guides men safely along the trail of war. In the Ancient Days he promised never to allow lightning to strike a honey locust tree. His promise to the Seven Clans had never before been broken. But that night it seemed that Thunder had abandoned our warriors, and that was why the women wailed.

On the day after, word spread among the children of the town that the tree had burned completely away, that there were no charred pieces, only a scattering of white ashes. Who had ever heard of such a thing? It must have certainly been an omen. Some of the older girls among us, their fears revived, began to wail anew. But I was too young. I went off with girls my own age and we played that we were married and that our husbands had been killed on the war trail. We wailed and mourned, but for us it was only play. Nothing more.

The third omen did not come until the following summer. On the day it happened, almost everyone was away at the ball ground watching the warriors play stickball. It was Mink who left the game and went back alone to the empty town. When he entered the palisade he noticed that there was no smoke rising from the townhouse. No smoke where there had always been smoke before. He hurried into the townhouse and found Shaker crying and beating his head against a post. In the hearth the Ancient Fire had died; there was nothing but charred wood, cold and black, no smoke, no heat, no breath of fire.

"My beloved older brother!" gasped Mink. "The fire is out!"

Shaker nodded, moaning, beating his head still harder until Mink ran to him and pulled him away from the post.

"How did it happen, my older brother?"

"I was not asleep," groaned Shaker. "I was sitting with the fire just as I should have been. Look at the wood! Look at it there. I didn't starve the fire. You can see the wood. You can see it for yourself. You can see that it was burning. I was not sleeping! I did not let it burn out!"

"I can see the wood. I can see that it was burning."

"It was burning, but then I realized it was starting to die. And yet it was nothing alarming. I went over and stirred it a bit. I didn't want it burning too much, just enough. But the coals kept fading, losing their heat as if they were being slowly smothered. I asked myself, What is this? and I added dry moss to bring up a flame. I put dry moss on hot coals and no flame came up. I blew and there was no flame. The coals still lost their heat. There was smoke and smoulder, but no flame. The moss was smothering it! I knocked it off and blew the coals. They glowed a little, but they were fading, dying. I put on some splinters, but they wouldn't light. I tried, but they would not light. I was the keeper of Ancient Fire. I was the keeper. . . ." Shaker moaned and rocked.

"It didn't die because of you," Mink said to him gently. "It was something else, something beyond you. There was nothing you could have done."

"I was the keeper!" Shaker began to bite at his own arm, drawing blood. Mink stopped him and pulled him to his feet.

"Come with me, my older brother. Come with me to visit my mother."

The town was empty that day. All of us were at the ball ground, all except the sick and the very old. Mink's mother was old, too old to leave her bed. She was alone in her house with Trotting Wolf, Mink's nephew, who had been given the task that day of watching over his grandmother. Trotting Wolf was only fourteen at the time. He was not happy to be missing the ball game. As he later told me, he thought Mink had come to relieve him.

Mink took Shaker into the house and sat him down.

"Here is Shaker, my mother. He has come to visit you."

Mink's mother was extremely old. As she peered at Shaker from her bed, her small head shook slowly back and forth. Her voice was soft and tremulous.

"It is good that you have come," she said.

"Trotting Wolf is leaving now," said Mink. "Shaker will stay here with you. He will take care of you until we return."

Shaker looked up at Mink.

"I am entrusting you with the care of my mother," said Mink. "She must have someone with her. I am sure no man would do himself violence before the eyes of such a venerable old woman."

Shaker bowed his head. Mink and Trotting Wolf left the house. Outside, Mink said, "Something terrible has happened, my nephew. Ancient Fire has died in the townhouse hearth. Shaker was the keeper and he blames himself, but it seems not to have been his fault. I am going back to the ball ground now to tell Gray Hawk and the people, but you must stay here and watch to see that Shaker does not try to leave your grandmother's house. I am afraid of what he might do. Don't let him see you or he will realize that he doesn't have to be sitting there with your grandmother."

"I'll try to keep him safe," said Trotting Wolf. "But what does it mean that the fire has died?"

Mink shook his head. "I don't know," he said. "I don't know what it means."

He left Trotting Wolf and went out of the town, down through the valley, and along the river to another valley, much smaller than ours, a flat expanse of bottom land where the ball game was being played.

The day Ancient Fire died in the townhouse, my brother Two Crows was the hero of the ball game. While Shaker was weeping and beating his head, I was laughing and cheering as my warrior brother carried the ball six times through the goal for our team from Quail Town. Once that day, he even got turned around in the fray and began running the wrong way, carrying the ball toward Bear Hill's goal. We laughed and screamed as the Bear Hill team helped him through. His own teammates tried to reach him to wrestle him to the ground. But suddenly he realized his mistake and spun around and raced all the way back to the Quail Town goal, hurling the ball through with his ball sticks and scoring a point. All the cheers were for my brother. I could hardly take my eyes from him. Two Crows, the finest warrior on the ball field, the swiftest, the most cunning, the most good-natured, the favorite.

My eyes were so fixed upon him that I did not realize anything was happening until he himself noticed it. Then I looked where he was looking and saw Gray Hawk and several beloved men hurrying from the ball ground toward the town. I saw the game officials standing together on the ball field with Mink in the center. Then the head official for the Quail Town team left the others and walked to the center of the field and raised his arms for silence.

"Quail Town must call an end to the game," he announced. "At this moment we are ahead, but all of us know that the game has not been played to the finish. We know that a team often comes from behind to score the winning point. Therefore we give the game to Bear Hill. The spoils of victory are theirs."

Not a sound was heard on the ball ground, not a whisper, not a question. In dreadful silence we waited to hear why such a thing was happening. But child that I was, my distress was not for any impending news of calamity, but for the loss of the shell ear pins I had bet on the game. I had put my faith in Two Crows when I had added these, the finest of my possessions, to the wager piles at the edge of the field. It had never occurred to me that I would lose them, and now I wanted to creep over and snatch them back before the Bear Hill people took them away. But I forgot my ear pins and everything else when Turtleback went onto the field and began to speak, for even a child such as I knew the meaning of Ancient Fire.

Turtleback was too old to speak loudly, and we strained to hear his words. "Seven Clans of Quail Town! You are my grandchildren, most of you, and some of you are my nieces and my nephews, and even a few are here, white upon the head as I am, who are my brothers and my sisters. These few, like I, were born away from here, in Blue Valley, our mother town. We still remember how in our youth our parents brought us down the river to a new valley and built new houses and a palisade of timber, tall and secure, to protect us from our enemies. But at first we had no townhouse and no Ancient Fire. We would journey back to Blue Valley for our feasts and celebrations.

"In the fullness of time it fell to me to stay in Blue Valley to study with one of my mother's brothers who lived there, an uncle who possessed the deep knowledge of the Seven Clans, who had learned it from his uncle, and he from his, and so on back into the Ancient Days of our people. At the end of my study a townhouse was built at Quail Town and the coals of Ancient Fire were given to me by the headman of Blue Valley. He addressed me with these words:

" 'Quail Town now receives a fire of its own. It is like a baby jumping down from its mother's womb. For the first time it has a breath of its own. The Seven Clans of Quail Town have chosen you to be their headman. You are the keeper of the fire. It is for you and your brothers to guard the breath of your town until others are chosen by the Seven Clans to take your place.'

"Now my nephew Gray Hawk is your headman. He has been admired all around the circle for his fairness in guiding the council and for his reliance on the gray-haired wisdom of the beloved men. He and his brothers have been loved by you as they have faithfully kept the fire.

"Beloved people of the Seven Clans! My heart is in pain and my eyes are filled with tears! The breath has gone out of Quail Town! Our town lies in the valley like a corpse in its bed! There is no heartbeat in the center! The fire has gone out!"

There was no outburst from the people. No wailing as on the night the warriors' tree had burned. Loved ones drew quietly into clusters and clung to each other, and on many faces there were tears.

The next one who spoke was the headman from Bear Hill. His speech was very short.

"Brothers and sisters of Quail Town. We tremble and weep with you in your misfortune. We are kinsmen of the same Seven Clans. We will not claim from you the spoils of a victory we have not won. There has been no victory on this day. Let each go home with what he brought."

And so the ball ground was soon empty, and we were walking back to the town. A few of the women began softly wailing, but there was, overall, a calm. Husband stayed beside wife, and child beside parent; yet each was alone with a cold, dark fear, and many were whispering to themselves, "What does it mean?"

The council met day after day. Every aspect of the thing was discussed. There were many at first who blamed Shaker, believing that he had slept. Gray Hawk declined to lead the council because, as he said, "A man must answer for the act of his brother." It was debated whether to choose another headman, but when consensus was at last reached, Shaker was exonerated and Gray Hawk was persuaded to resume his position of leadership. But for Shaker it was too late. He could not bring himself to lift his head and walk among us. I can still remember the day I heard that he was dead, that he had pushed an arrow into his own heart.

The council grimly carried on. They considered whether or not to abandon the town. There were some who felt that this would be the safest course. But our valley was very fertile and well-situated, and most of us loved it too much to leave. And so it was decided that the townhouse and all the houses of the people would be cleansed and the bark taken from the frames and burned and we would begin anew. Some, like my parents, burned even the frames of their houses and started over completely. Old Turtleback was sent to Blue Valley with Gray Hawk and the beloved men, and they brought back Ancient Fire and placed it in the townhouse. The beloved men then decreed that a new town had been born. We called it Mulberry Town. But of the two hundred people who had been living in Quail Town, there were perhaps thirty who did not join the consensus. Quietly withdrawing from the council, they gathered together their things and moved back up the river to live in Blue Valley.

The last omen, like the first, was also seen by Mink alone. It was the fourth, the completion, the closing of a circle around that which was foretold. But there was no one in the Seven Clans with power enough to see into the circle. No one knew what was there. "It is a black circle," the priests would say, but even I knew that, and I was but a child.

When Mink saw the fourth omen, he was downriver near Bear Hill, traveling off the paths gathering herbs and roots for medicine. He came to a large clearing in the forest, a place known to most of our hunters for the deer that could often be found there. He squatted at the edge of the forest to dig a root, and when he looked up again, he saw Immortals standing together in the clearing. How many were there he could not say. They looked to him like ordinary people of the Seven Clans, but he knew they were spirit people because they had appeared so suddenly. He nodded to them, but decided to stay away from them. One can never be sure about Immortals. Usually they are friendly. But they can sometimes be mischievous.

So Mink stood back from them and watched. A herd of deer came into the clearing. Then, to his surprise, the Immortals went among the herd and began to leap onto the backs of the deer, and the deer began to run about the clearing carrying the Immortals on their backs. The Immortals looked at Mink and laughed at him. Yet there were some who were weeping—there were some who looked at him and mourned. The herd bolted suddenly from the clearing, carrying away the Immortals as they ran. Mink tried to follow them through the forest, but they left no trail, no tracks of any kind, and he soon gave up and went back to the town.

When the Seven Clans were told of this, they were afraid, for they knew that a circle of omens had been completed. More of our townsmen, about twenty in all, packed their things and moved up the river to Blue Valley. They did not know then that in all the mountains and valleys of the Cherokees, in all the land of the Seven Clans, there would be no sanctuary.

TWO

I sat in the doorway of our house and watched the storm. Cold weather was behind us, the trees in full leaf. It was not the season to be inside. But a blowing rain had swirled through the open sides of the summer cookshed, driving us from the yard into our houses.

"Wet wood," muttered Cougar Woman. I glanced around and watched my grandmother poke at the fire. The smoke was awful, as if the rain were beating it back through the smoke hole.

"Perhaps Quail Moccasin has some that is dry," said Day Moon, my mother, kneeling by the hearth, sitting back on her bare feet the way women are supposed to sit. Her knee-length skirt of deerskin was tucked neatly around her legs. Her hair, shiny with bear oil, was turned into a careful knot at the back of her neck. She wore shell ear pins through the lobes of her ears, and above her low-hanging breasts was a necklace of shell beads, stark white and lovely against her dark, copper skin. Day Moon always looked exactly as a woman should, and I admired her for it and watched her closely, trying to learn the way of it. With me there was always a skirt turning sideways or wisps of hair coming loose and hanging down in disarray. I was more like my grandmother, Cougar Woman, who even now, bent over the fire, was forever pushing back a lock of white hair from her face. Outside there was a flash of lightning, and I turned back to watch the storm, to listen to the thunder rumble through the mountains.

"Every time we get enough girls for a swim, it rains," I complained. "It's the omens. Thunder has turned his back on us."

I had come to my eleventh year with too much worry, with too much blackness in my childish dreaming. It was the omens. To me they meant that every bad thing I imagined would surely happen.

"Omens," said my mother. "Everything that goes wrong is because of the omens. Nothing is anyone's fault any more. If a hunter comes in empty-handed, it's the omens. If a woman ruins a firing of pottery, it's the omens. Your brother Little Buck even claims to have lost a race yesterday because of the omens. As if someone did not have to lose."

"But it has rained every time we've been ready to go swimming. Every single time."

"It is the rainy season, my daughter. You don't need omens to tell you that it will rain in early summer. But here now, you should not be so discouraged. When it stops, you will have your fun. You be sure to stay with the group."

"I will." I watched her as she rose and came over to me, bringing a half-finished basket and a bundle of split cane, some of it dyed red and black.

"A woman's hands are never idle," she said as she handed it all to me. Then she went back to the fire and picked up the strap for carrying wood and took her deerskin cape from the post where it hung and put it over her head. Ducking by me out the door, she ran through the rain to her sister's house next to ours.

"I'm a girl," I said sullenly.

"You will be a woman soon enough," said my grandmother. "With a woman's thoughts and a woman's chores. Men don't marry lazy women."

I took one of the cane splits and began weaving it slowly into the basket. What was the use in having a husband? He would just die on the war trail and leave me grieving. That was what the omens said.

I knew death. I knew how it snatched away friends and family. Two years ago it had taken my brother Talks Walking. He was fourteen years old and strong and healthy. Then suddenly he was ill, and just as suddenly he was dead. Perhaps it was sorcery, an enemy within the palisade, though no accusation was ever made.

Talks Walking had died before the omens. It was the others I worried about now. Especially Two Crows. He was a warrior, and this summer he would go back on the war trail. Last summer, the summer after the tree had burned, no one had wanted to lead a war party; no one had wanted to be responsible for losing men. But the war priest went into seclusion and fasted and divined until he said he had discovered why Thunder had turned his back, and then he went to the river and worked and conjured until he had brought Thunder around to face us again. Some people wondered if he had been successful, but most of the warriors thought he had, and now war parties would probably go out before the summer passed.

I not only feared for Two Crows' life on the war trail. I also worried what might happen to us in the town if too many warriors went away and left us unprotected. I could see us sleeping in the pre-dawn darkness, a Coosa raiding party slipping up to the town on the downwind side, no barking from the dogs, our enemies climbing the bastions without a sound, clubbing the guards in silence. Then over the wall and into the town, screaming death, wild paint and war clubs, bursting into our house, my father on his feet in desperate battle, Little Buck fighting as if he were a man, my mother screaming, my grandmother grabbing up a spear and rushing into the battle. But there would be too many against us and one by one we would fall, my grandmother clubbed and scalped, then my mother, then Little Buck, and finally my father, all dead but me.

A Coosa warrior would take me as his captive, a slave girl for his wife, but outside I would escape and hide in the darkness. I would crawl beneath a granary and pull dead dogs over me to keep from being seen, and there I would stay through the following day, grieving and waiting for Two Crows to come home and find me.

"I thought you were the one who wanted to go swimming," said my grandmother.

Back to reality. The rain had stopped. "I am," I said. "I'm going now. This basket. I was so busy working on it."

"Yes, I can see you did a lot." She was smiling, but it was not to shame me, and I did not feel ashamed. Cougar Woman was very good about letting things go by. "Stay with the group," she said. "You had better hurry and catch up."

I ducked outside and ran through the streets, bare feet slapping down with quick splashes on the rain-soaked ground. I passed by yards with flat baskets of wild plums newly brought out to dry in the sun, with dogs shaking dry and small children playing in puddles, with women bringing their work back out into the open. Then I came to the open plaza and looked around. Two women were nearby, standing and talking, and one of them said to me, "Are you looking for the girls, my child? They've already gone. You'd better hurry."

"Thank you, my mother."

"Stay with the group," the other called after me.

I went around the plaza and between the houses on the other side and out through the palisade entrance. There they were, almost halfway across the valley, a group of girls, with two women to look after them. They were heading for the line of trees that screened the river and the deep hole in the bend that was good for swimming. They were skipping along, shouting and laughing, and I set out at a run to catch them. But soon I slowed to a walk. What did it matter? With the girls in front of me, the guards on the palisade behind, and open cornfield in between, I was as safe as I could ever be. I would meet them at the river. In the meanwhile it was a lovely day. The summer rain had made it so. Mist was rising warm and steamy from the wetness of the earth. The corn, already as high as my knee, was a deep, healthy green, and young bean vines were winding up the stalks. Birds were everywhere, singing from their hearts. I could see tiny warblers swaying on the corn, fluffing their feathers to dry in the warm summer sun. It was a day to be alive in, to forget about omens and screaming death.

I crossed the valley breathing deeply, feeling happy. Close by the place where the girls had entered the trees, I heard the call of a dove. I stopped and listened, and it came again. *Gule-hoo-hoo-hoo.* So beautiful. Sometimes a little sad. From this my name had come—Rain Dove—a dove calling after the summer rain. I looked about me at the steamy blue and green, the world washed clean, the warm air filled with sunshine and birdsong, and the dove calling after the summer rain.

Then something in that moment seized me, something new, something I had never realized before. *I could die.* My life could end. There had been rain doves before I was born and named for them, and if I were to die, there would still be rain doves. There would still be all of this—beauty and rain and birds and corn—and summers—it would all go on without me. *I could die.* Those terrible omens! They warned us of something horrible, something black. We could all die. If enemies could kill my family, they could kill me too. *Dead.* Black death.

I looked at the world and it was not beautiful anymore. It was frightening, and quiet. Too quiet. I could no longer hear the girls ahead of me. Why could I not hear them? What was happening? Had there been enemies hiding in the woods?

I looked toward the trees in terror. Then I turned and fled for my life back across the cornfield. With every step I felt an arrow in my back. I stumbled and fell. Crying out, I burst into sobs. I scrambled to my feet and ran, blinded by my tears, pushing my legs as fast as they would go, running for the safety of the palisade. Then when I was close to it, I stopped. There was the palisade, and there was the guard, and he was not giving the cry of alarm. I looked behind me. There was no one there, no one chasing. I had imagined it all. How foolish I must look. Could the guard have seen me crying? Perhaps not. Perhaps he thought I had forgotten something. Yes, that was it. I hit my hand against my head, berating myself. You stupid frog, I scolded, you forgot it. Now you have to go home and get it. And you are crazy to think you can get back to the river in time. You might as well forget swimming for today. You might as well go home and find something else to do.

I was acting it out as best I could, wiping my tears dry, hoping my face was not ruined with splotches, trying desperately to think of something I could have forgotten. I crossed the log bridge over the ditch and started through the entrance of the palisade.

"Rain Dove!"

I looked up in confusion, and there he was on the bastion —Two Crows, of all people. He was the guard. He had been the one to see that foolish episode. I felt my face burning, flaming hot, and I could not speak.

"Come up and talk to me, my little sister."

"I . . . uh. . . ." I pointed toward home. "I forgot something."

"Oh, come on up. It's a fine day. You should see the world from up here. Come on, I'll give you a hand."

I knew I could not fool Two Crows. By the time I got to the top, my lower lip was quivering.

"What is it, little one?" he asked. "What frightened you out there?"

"The girls who went swimming," I stammered, my voice breaking into sobs. "I couldn't hear them anymore. Do you think they've been killed?"

"No," Two Crows said gently. "They haven't been killed. We searched the trees before they went in, up and down the river. There is no one in there but the girls—and maybe a few possums."

I had to smile at that. I wiped at my eyes and tried to stop crying. "Why couldn't I hear them, then?"

"I'll bet they were playing the quiet game," said Two Crows.

"Do you think so? Maybe they were."

"We'll watch for them and see. We'll see if any come out of the woods carrying broken twigs." In the quiet game, there were no winners, only losers. Anyone who broke a twig in the quiet game had to pick it up and carry it with him for the rest of the day. It was very funny to see it, and very embarrassing to have to do it.

I stood with Two Crows and we looked out across the valley. It was beautiful now, as it had been before. For a long time we were silent, until at last I said, "What do the omens mean? I wish someone could tell me what they mean."

"You're too young to be worrying about such things."

"I'm old enough for my hands not to be idle."

He looked at me, but did not say anything.

"Do the omens mean we are all going to die?"

"No, my little sister, they don't mean that. How could such a thing happen?"

"Our enemies."

"Kill every one of us? That never happens. To lose even five or ten is something terrible. There are not even any stories about a whole town getting killed. The worst story I've ever heard was fifty people, and I doubt that it was true."

"Fifty people!" I cried.

"But there are three times as many people living here. Fifty people is not everybody."

"Fifty dead people!"

"It's a story! It's a story, little one. What is this with you? You are getting so upset about things. Fifty people is only a story. I mention it because it is the worst thing I have ever heard to have happened anywhere. If it happened here, it would be bad, but it would not be the end of everything. And I don't think it or anything like it will happen here. Do you want to know what I think about the omens?"

"What?"

"I think we will never know what they mean. We are all being so careful now, that whatever was supposed to have happened will never come about. That is the way I see it."

I thought about it for a moment. "I like that. It's better. It's a lot better. I hope everybody keeps on being very careful."

"Look there," said Two Crows. Across the valley the girls were coming into the cornfield from the trees. "Do you think they have been playing the quiet game?"

"I don't know. They're too far away. What do you think? Can you see?"

"No, not yet . . . yes. What is that? Is that Fawn?" He was starting to chuckle.

"Yes, it is Fawn," I grinned. "What is it? It looks like . . . a greenbrier vine!"

"How did she make a noise with that?"

I was laughing too much to answer.

"Maybe she scraped against it with her skirt," he said.

"Or stepped on it," I squeaked, "and yelled."

We doubled up with hilarity, laughing, groaning, stamping our feet, holding our sides; tears streamed down my brother's face as well as mine. Two Crows was like that. Fierce and manly on the trail of war, yet gentle enough to look at the world with a child of eleven years and see all the fear and all the humor that was there.

Two Crows cheered me for the day. But in the darkness of the nights that followed, lying awake in my bed, I could not still my thoughts, and often I would cry, burying my face in my blanket, trying hard not to be heard. But I was heard, and my family grew concerned. They talked. It was decided that I needed a sister for a while, someone my own age to be with all the time. My clan sisters, the daughters of my mother's sisters, were all too old or too young. At last it was decided that I should spend the rest of the summer in the house of my father's sister, Turkey Woman. There I could be with Fawn, my father's niece. We could play together, eat together, work and sleep together, and I would forget about omens and other disturbing things and begin to enjoy myself again.

Fawn and I called each other sister. When I was very small, I thought she was my real sister. The matter of how people are related is confusing for a young child because no one takes the trouble to explain things. But in time the child learns that there are real kinsmen, all in his mother's line, and other people he calls kinsmen who are not related to him at all. Only the people in his own clan, his mother's clan, are real kinsmen, yet he speaks to all the others as if they were, because in a way all the town is like one family, and all stand beside each other against the world outside.

Yet things are not always so close within the palisade walls. If one man wrongs another or takes a life, then there will be a hardness between their two clans, a darkening of hearts, and there is no more calling each other brother and sister until the matter is set straight and brought into balance.

But though I was a daughter of the Bird clan and Fawn a daughter of my father's Wolf clan, yet it had never made any difference between us. We were always very close and there had never been a time when we did not call each other sister.

It was exciting for me to bundle up my things and move to Turkey Woman's house on the other side of the plaza. There, in a new house, with a new pattern of living, with Fawn as my constant companion, I did forget about omens and dark things. Turkey Woman kept us busy. Fawn and I were growing less childish every day, and we were expected to do our share of the work. Turkey Woman had us making baskets of every size and cane mats for sitting on and for covering walls and doorways. She helped us tan skins and make leggings and moccasins, skirts, capes, and breechcloths. She showed us how to separate the fibers from the bark of mulberry trees and make it into beautiful white cloth. And when we thought we could not work another moment, she would know it and send us out with Fawn's clan sisters to pick blackberries, with one or two of Fawn's mothers to look after us.

I hardly had a chance to miss my family. My father, Cries Victory, came often to visit. Turkey Woman was his sister, his actual sister, and her children were his special responsibility. My father had another sister and a brother, but they had been among those who moved to Blue Valley after the town-house fire went out. I think it pained my father that his brother had moved away from him. But he had many clan brothers. It was not as if he had been left alone.

My brother Two Crows also visited frequently. Someone who did not know better might have assumed that he was coming to see Running By, Fawn's older brother, who was a warrior like Two Crows. But those two had never been great friends. Two Crows came to see Crazy Eyes, our father's father, who lived there in Turkey Woman's house. Crazy Eyes was a fine old man, and he and Two Crows were very fond of each other. I think perhaps Crazy Eyes liked Two Crows more than he liked Running By, and that did not help things between the two warriors.

The only unpleasant part of living with Fawn was Bluejay, the younger of her two brothers. He was just a little older than we were, about the age of my own brother, Little Buck. With Bluejay it was always, "Watch me!" or "Me first!" He not only boasted, he lied, claiming daring feats he had never done. But perhaps the worst thing about Bluejay was that he had a temper he could not control. It was very strong in him to be the best in everything, and if he lost a contest of any kind, his anger would flare and he would not try to hide it. To the boy who had just bested him, it was a serious insult, an insinuation by Bluejay that the winner had taken some manner of unfair advantage. It often caused hard feelings. The older Bluejay grew, the more serious were the situations he created. My father did his best to handle it. Several times he had long talks with Bluejay and tried to show him that the path he was following was a bent path, that it was not the path to manhood. But Bluejay's ears were closed, and my father's words were blown away on the wind. My dislike for Bluejay increased when after one of these talks I overheard him speaking spitefully about my father to Running By. Running By was his older brother. It was Running By's place to make clear to his younger brother that a nephew does not speak harshly about his uncle, especially if the uncle is trying in every way to guide the nephew into manhood. But Running By was only a little less obnoxious than Bluejay; he let the younger brother speak harshly without reproach. There were many times when I regretted that my father's brother had moved away to Blue Valley and left him to struggle alone with these two nephews.

When Bluejay fell ill that summer, he had no one to blame except himself. He was guilty of spitting into the fire. He befouled the power and purity of the fire, and he boasted to the boys with him that he had done it because he was not afraid, because he had power so great that he could throw back any ill effects that might come from it. But the boys called him crazy and drew away from him and went home without him because they did not want to be associated in any way with such foolhardiness. When Cries Victory and his clan brothers learned of it, they called their nephew to them and asked if it were true. Bluejay laughed and said it was a joke. He said he had not really spit into the fire, that he had made fools of his friends and caused them to be frightened over nothing. But when he fell ill, his uncles knew that he had lied. He had spit into the fire, boasted of a power he did not have, then lied without shame to his uncles. It was a wonder to me that he did not die from his illness.

My father was very concerned and stayed with Bluejay day and night, for though the boy was troublesome, he was still my father's nephew, and a man will always love best his own blood and bone. The first curer called in was a young priest who had been known to have had success in curing various illnesses caused by fire. He worked four days with Bluejay, but there were no signs of improvement. So the young curer took the two deerskins paid to him by my father and went home.

"Mink is the one who can cure the boy," said old Crazy Eyes. Bluejay's father was there and he agreed. Neither of these two were in the Wolf clan, but Cries Victory listened to them nonetheless, and he sent Running By to ask Mink to come.

Mink was a man of great power, the only one among the Seven Clans to have seen the complete circle of omens. Fawn and I were awed that he should be coming to her house. We wanted to get a close look at this extraordinary man and hear him talk to our own two fathers and to our grandfather. We would have even envied Bluejay his position in the center of things except that he looked so pale and miserable, and except that the presence of so powerful a curer implied the presence of a similarly powerful illness.

But when Mink arrived, he appeared to be less than we had expected. He was dressed like an ordinary man, in a breechcloth and a short cape of deerskin. His feet were bare, and in the stretched flesh-loop of each earlobe he wore an ear spool made not of copper or shell, but of mere wood. His only mark of distinction was the four eagle feathers hanging down from the crown of his head. One feather for each omen, I thought. I had expected his eyes to be filled with deep mystery, but they were not. I had expected him to speak with firmness and authority, but he spoke instead with a kindly thoughtfulness. He was just a little older than my father, so he called my father younger brother, though they were not real brothers. He called Crazy Eyes uncle, and that was a real kinship, for Crazy Eyes, like Mink, was of the Deer clan. Although Mink was no real kinsman of either of us, Fawn and I called him our uncle. Yet that is not to say that we felt free to speak to him. We sat so quietly that I do not think he even noticed we were there. He stayed only a short time, examining Bluejay and asking questions of him. Then he spoke briefly to Cries Victory and to Crazy Eyes. Cries Victory gave him several deerskins and a pouch of tobacco, and he left.

He returned the next morning before dawn. He boiled medicine in a pot on the fire, then sent the rest of us out of the house, leaving him alone with Bluejay. Turkey Woman built a fire in the cookshed. We gathered around it and listened to the rattle of the medicine gourd and to the murmur of the song that came from inside the house. Dawn pressed into the eastern sky, spreading light across the hills, glowing red at first and then fading into gold and blue daylight. There was a warmth and cheerfulness among us, a comfortable feeling that Mink was indeed the one who could cure Bluejay.

For four days he worked, from dawn until noon. The fourth day completed the circle, and Mink announced that Bluejay would recover. Then he went out and sat in the yard with Cries Victory and Crazy Eyes, the three of them smoking tobacco and speaking together, friendly and relaxed. I was working nearby and could hear their conversation. And I saw before they did my brother Two Crows coming into the yard.

"Now, here is my son," Cries Victory exclaimed with pleasure.

"My grandchild, it is good that you have come," said Crazy Eyes.

"I hope that you will sit with us, my nephew," said Mink.

Two Crows sat down with them and they passed the pipe to him. He acknowledged each one around the circle. "My grandfather. My uncle. My father. It is good to find each of you here."

They smoked in silence, in the thoughtful calm that allows a situation to settle and come into balance. After a time, Two Crows said, "We have a visitor at the townhouse."

"Most interesting," said Crazy Eyes. "I wonder where he comes from."

"From the Lower River, my grandfather."

"Bringing shell?"

"A little. They were trading when I left."

"And does he also bring good news from his people?" asked Mink.

"He says that their crops are very good this year. Already their corn is filling out."

"It is warmer down there," said Cries Victory. "They plant earlier."

"He says they will have their New Corn Festival on the new of the moon. He says that we are welcome, as always. Any of us who wants to come will be welcome as their guests."

"It is too far for me," said Crazy Eyes. "I am content to wait for our own corn to ripen. But some of the younger ones might want to go down. A few went last year."

"I would like to see the ocean," said Two Crows.

"It is worth the trip to see the ocean," said Mink. "From where they are on the Lower River, it is only two days by water."

Crazy Eyes lit up the pipe and it went around the circle again.

"They lost a woman to the Coosas," said Two Crows.

"Captured?" said Mink.

"Killed."

"It is a hard thing," said Cries Victory.

"She was keeping the birds out of one of the cornfields most distant from the town. It was in the spring when the first sprouts were coming up, and she was watching with an old grandfather. It was as if the enemy appeared from nowhere. She was clubbed and scalped in an instant. They held the old man and debated what to do with him. He taunted them, naming off the ones of their people he had killed and then naming the ones his brothers had killed, and then his nephews. He was full of courage, that old man, and he wanted them to kill him. But they let him go so that he could tell his people who had killed their sister."

"I doubt that he really wanted them to kill him," said Crazy Eyes. "The older I get, the more I doubt such things."

The others chuckled.

"I suppose the people got revenge," said Mink.

"They chased the war party, but they could not catch them. So the woman's brothers got together a party of their own. They went deep into Coosa territory and captured a woman and brought her back and adopted her into their clan in their dead sister's place."

"It is good to see the Coosas made fools of," said my father. "I'm glad they struck deep."

"Does the Coosa woman give them trouble?" asked Mink.

"She doesn't try to get back to her home. It is too far. She grieved at first, of course, but she is getting used to her new family. They treat her well."

"A captive woman can be made content," said Crazy Eyes. "It is not easy, but I have seen it."

"She is content enough to tell stories. She told an interesting one from the south. It comes from the people who live farthest to the south, so I suppose it passed around the circle in quite a few townhouses before it reached the Coosa townhouses."

"A man in my grandfather's time once traveled south and south until he reached the farthest edge of the land," said Crazy Eyes. "He said that it becomes so warm that there is no longer any winter. None to speak of. And the plants change. Imagine that. In the farthest places the plants are not the same."

"They have different spirit people, too," said Two Crows. "That is what the woman's story was about. She told the Lower River People that in the farthest places south they have Immortals that live in townhouses on the ocean and make their clothing out of copper. And strangest of all, they eat the same food that ordinary people eat. The very same food. Corn and beans and squash and meat."

It was just then that Running By came home. He joined the group. I knew he was angry that Two Crows had gotten there first and had told the best parts of the news. They passed the pipe around and soon the conversation was going again, more lively now, the way talk will be when there is rivalry. But I noticed that Mink was no longer entering into the discussion. I noticed that he had become silent and thoughtful.

THREE

It was a warm fall day with just a little coolness in the breeze. It was to be a day of games, of contests at the ball ground, a day of wagers and cheering, of fun and good food. It was a day that began with laughter. I was in the cookshed in our yard, filling a basket with chestnut bread. I heard my father in our house, the soft murmur of his voice and then his hearty laughter, and my mother laughing through her hands, I could tell, laughing with her face covered. Then my grandmother came out waving her hands.

"Those two are indecent!" she exclaimed. "Too much for an old woman. My daughter lets him talk like that in front of her mother. The two of them, carrying on like young lovers."

I laughed, wondering exactly how that was, how it would be to be a young lover.

"She is too shameless for me," said Cougar Woman. "I'll walk alone to the ball ground."

"Walk with me," I said. "I'm finished here."

She protested. "What would Blue Shoes think if you arrived with an old woman?"

"He would say, Look at that! What a beautiful grandmother she has. So sensuous!"

"Ah!" said Cougar Woman in disgust, but I knew she was pleased. I picked up the basket, heavy with the boiled bread cakes, and we started toward the palisade entrance. She said, "Will you bet on Two Crows in the shooting?"

"I haven't decided. Do you suppose his feelings would be hurt if I bet on someone else? Blue Shoes, maybe?"

"You should bet on Blue Shoes if you want. Two Crows understands things. He is a good brother."

"I know," I said. "I'll miss him if he marries Rising Moon."

"And you think he will?"

"Someday."

"And you will marry Blue Shoes?"

"I am too young to marry."

"Fourteen is young, but not too young."

"How old were you?"

"Sixteen," said my grandmother. "A good age."

"My mother was nineteen."

"Ah! I thought she would never marry. I kept saying to her, Forget about Cries Victory. He is too busy winning war names. He has no time for a wife."

"Just like Two Crows."

"Like Two Crows. His father's son."

"And like Blue Shoes," I said. "I am afraid he's turning out that way. I'm not so sure about him anymore. But I have been noticing Trapper. What do you think about him?"

"A very good-looking young man. Very handsome. But I don't know what kind of hunter he is."

We came to the palisade then and went out through the entrance of overlapping walls. There was no mistaking that it was a festival day. Many people were just outside the palisade, milling about, happy, waiting for friends. Cougar

Woman left me and joined a group of grandmothers. I found Fawn, and the two of us left together, going along the river trail, out of the valley and through the southern hills into the next valley, the small valley, not so far away, that was the ball ground. We went to the area near the river where the women had gathered, where huge cookpots steamed on fires, and we left our food there. Then we began to wander about the ball ground.

It was midmorning when the games began, first with a race, a long run the length of the field and back again. Fawn cheered for her brother Bluejay and I for my brother Little Buck, but neither of them won, though Little Buck did the better of the two. I could see that Bluejay was angry. He was always angry when he lost.

The shooting was next, and Fawn's other brother, Running By, was the first to come to the mark. He shot well, considering the distance, his first three arrows passing easily through the target. But with his opponents yelling louder than ever to spoil his shot, his fourth arrow went high and he was out of the contest.

Two Crows was the second one to shoot. He walked down the field and took his place at the mark. I glanced toward the target and saw Little Buck cross the field behind it, heading up the river trail toward home to take his turn as watchman on the palisade. I turned to watch Two Crows. He was already drawing back his first arrow. There was a great deal of noise, the warriors yelling, whooping, trying to spoil his aim. I saw his lips move, whispering a song to guide the arrow. Then the arrow was speeding away from him, and my eyes followed it, tracing its flight to the target.

Suddenly I saw what was going to happen. I screamed—I think I screamed. I grabbed Fawn and shook her, screaming, but it was like silence, silent fury, the world spinning, tumbling, and pitching me to my knees as Bluejay ran behind the target and the arrow passed through it and buried itself in his neck, blood spurting, and he clutched the arrow shaft and fell. I could see people running past me, crying out. And above it all I could hear the agony of Two Crows, my brother's cry of despair, a cry as much for himself as for Bluejay.

I do not remember getting to my feet, but I remember walking, and I remember my legs were shaking so badly that I reached out and held on to someone, never looking to see who it was. I knew I was going to the place where Bluejay had fallen. What else could I do? But I never saw him again. I saw his people gathered around him, and I knew that he lay in the midst of them and that his blood was running out onto the ground. I saw his mothers and sisters weeping and wailing. I saw Fawn with her hair hanging loose and tears streaming down her face. I began to cry. I saw Turkey Woman wailing pathetically and pushing her way to her son. And then I saw my father. I saw his agony. I saw him plunge through the crowd to his nephew, his own blood, shot and killed by his son whom he dearly loved but who was not his own blood, who was not his clansman. My father was a Wolf and Bluejay was a Wolf. Two Crows was a Bird.

Holding my hands against my mouth, I turned and ran, sobbing, running to Two Crows, my brother, my own brother who now would have to die. The Wolf people would rise as one and come to him and shoot an arrow through his heart. The Bird people could do nothing. We owed a life to the Wolf people. It was their duty to take it.

My sobs turned into moans and I ran without direction, in circles I think, until I tripped over some little child and knocked him down. When he began to cry, it brought me back to myself. I picked him up and stood him on his feet and stroked his hair and pressed my cheek against his, as if nothing in the world was more important than that he should stop crying. And when he did, I stood up and looked around. I saw the Wolf people gathered in a knot around Bluejay, and down the field I saw Two Crows. Little Buck was standing with him, and our clan brothers and our uncles. Near them was a group of women, Bird women, all weeping and wailing, and I knew my mother and my grandmother were among them. Between the two clans stood the other people of the town, wringing their hands, some crying, yet all knowing that it was not their affair, that there was nothing they could do. It had begun and it must finish. They left an opening in their midst, a clear path between the Wolf people and the Bird people.

I began to think about Bluejay and how much trouble he had always caused. I thought about Two Crows and how fine a warrior he was, how loved he was, how he had a woman he wanted to marry, how he had not meant to kill Bluejay, how it was not right that his life was finished. But we owed them a life and they would take it. It was their right, their duty. I looked at Two Crows in his despair. It was hideous to see him waiting to die.

It had become like a slow-moving nightmare. The Wolf people rose and turned, a single mass of anger and grief. I found myself moving to stand with Two Crows, not because it would matter, but because there was nothing else to do. I saw the Wolf people divide, the men stepping forward in vengeance. It was their duty. And it was our duty to step aside. But instead, we drew more closely together. The Wolf men stood facing us, and Running By came to the front and strung his bow. It was his brother who was dead, and the vengeance was to be his own.

But then Little Buck moved to stand in front of his own brother. Then our clan brothers came and stood beside Little Buck, and together they enclosed Two Crows in a circle; and I was standing with them, the only woman, accepted by them, or perhaps unnoticed. Our uncles came forward and stood in a line before us, and I thought to myself, Why are we doing this? We have no right.

Running By's brothers and uncles began to string their bows, and now my brothers and uncles were doing the same. A battle. It was to be a battle. It was wrong for us to turn it into a battle, and yet we were doing it. Then I saw that the men of the other five clans were stringing their bows and taking sides. Things were happening too quickly. The women raised their voices in battle song, urging their men to bravery. I stood in the midst of the men, weaponless and terror-stricken. I saw Running By set an arrow in his bowstring and pull it back and back, aiming it into our midst, and our men began to arm their bows. The battle was beginning.

Then all at once a man was standing between the two clans. It was Mink. He stood for a moment and then sat down on the ground, alone, and began to fill his pipe. The sun halted in the sky; nothing moved. Then Crazy Eyes came forward, grandfather of both clans, his old face streaked with tears, and he sat down beside Mink. I saw Running By's bowstring begin to relax, and I felt the terror fall away from me. Gray Hawk came forward next, stopping first to whisper to a young boy, who then ran off toward the cookfires. Others came and joined Mink. The boy soon returned with a coal, and Mink's pipe was lit and passed around the circle of beloved men. For a long time they smoked in silence, and we waited. Then they began to speak quietly among themselves. It went on and on. At last Mink got to his feet and began to speak.

"People of the Seven Clans. You are my kinsmen. We live together within the same palisade. We live together as one family. We live together as a people who are not ignorant. We are not barbarians. We know the ways of the world. We know that there is right and there is wrong. We know there is a straight path that is white and a bent path that is black. Today is a sorrowful day. We have seen a nephew of our town die before our eyes. And we have seen much more, we have experienced much more, and we know in our hearts that it has been dreadful and wrong. Let us send this day to the world of dreams and speak of it no more. Yet, let us not forget that one of us has died. A nephew of the Wolf clan died by the hand of a nephew of the Bird clan. We all know what is right. The spirit of the dead must not be left to wander on this side of the Darkening Land. It is the duty of the Wolf clan to avenge this death. It is the duty of the Bird clan to stand aside and let it be done. Yet the gray-headed men believe that this day has seen enough sorrow. Let each of us return now to his home. Tomorrow is soon enough to set the matter straight. Let the men of the two clans agree upon the time and place, and let the Bird clan face with courage that from which there is no escape."

There was much weeping as we went home. I walked alone, looking down at the ground, aching, blinking back the tears whenever they began to come. I tried to hold on to what Mink had said, for if the thing were so inevitable, then courage was all that was left for us.

All the people of the Bird clan came to our house. They

came in silence, and no one looked at anyone else. There were soon too many of us crowded together, and two of my clan sisters took the children to another house. Then it was suggested that the women should also go to a place of their own, that the men could discuss things better without so much crying. When the men promised to send word continuously of everything that was said, the women agreed to leave. My mother was suffering from so much grief that she could hardly walk, and they were almost carrying her from the house. I myself refused to go, and this small thing was seized upon as a point of great contention. But Two Crows ended it.

"She stood with the men before," he said. "Let her be." It was the first time he had spoken since it all began, and everyone fell silent.

The rest of the women left, and the men sat down, some on the beds against the walls, some around the fire in the center of the room. No further attention was paid to me. They smoked, each man from his own pipe. For a long time they thought about things and did not speak as each struggled to bring the necessary calm to his own mind.

At last one of my uncles said, simply, "How could it have happened?"

"Bluejay was coming after me," said Little Buck.

Startled, we turned and looked at him.

He began to explain. "We had wagered against each other on the race. I told him beforehand that I had to leave after the race to take my turn watching on the palisade and there would be no chance for the loser to win back what he lost. He said it made no difference. But I should have known better. We wagered ear spools, and when I won, Bluejay became angry. I should never have placed the bet with him. I should have known. I tried to give the ear spools back, but he would not have me give him anything. He insisted that I stay and bet again, on the shooting. I told him that my uncle was waiting for me to come take his place on the bastion, but that I would stay anyway, just long enough for his brother to shoot. If Running By put all four arrows through the target, Bluejay would win back his ear spools. If he missed I would keep them. Bluejay thought it was a good idea until Running By missed with that last arrow. Now he wanted still another chance, but I took the ear spools and left. I think he was coming after me when he was hit. I know he was angry. He must have forgotten everything else, even the shooting. When I heard the cries, I turned back and saw what had happened." Little Buck dropped his head. "I think perhaps it is I who deserves to die."

"You did nothing wrong," said Two Crows.

"I did as much as you."

"No. It was my arrow, shot from my bow, by my hand."

"Two Crows is right. He is the first cause," said Four Paws, my mother's brother, the headman of our clan. He had not been at the ball ground that day. He had been the one on the palisade whose place Little Buck was supposed to have taken. "We acted shamefully today," he said.

"The rest of us, my elder brother, but not you," said another of my uncles.

"If I had been there, I would have been standing with you. And yet it was wrong. If it had not been stopped, how many would have been killed? It would have been a horrible thing, and the blame would have been upon each of us. But the disaster we invited did not occur, and so perhaps we can put aside for a moment the question of right and wrong. As a practical matter, we may have benefited from our action. We have gained time. My younger brothers, my nephews, I suggest that we offer to dry up the tears of the Wolf clan with goods instead of blood. There are now two reasons for them to hear us. The first is what we have just learned, that Bluejay was acting wrongly toward the Bird clan when he was killed. The second is Cries Victory. He will not want to see his kinsmen take the life of his son."

"I think there is no use in asking," said Two Crows. "It is Running By who wants my blood. He is the brother, and they will listen to him."

"But he will listen to his uncle," said Four Paws.

"He is not the best of nephews," replied Two Crows.

"I think you are too discouraged," said Four Paws. "Little Buck and I will go to the beloved men and tell our story and ask them to speak for us to the Wolf clan. Surely Running By will listen to the beloved men."

Word was sent to the women, and they agreed that this was the best course. Four Paws and Little Buck hurried away. A feeling of relief began to spread through the house. The men began to talk among themselves, and there was even light laughter here and there. Some of the women joined us, my grandmother among them, and she came and sat beside me. I tried to give her an encouraging smile.

"I wish *I* had stood with the men," she said.

"No, it was crazy."

"Everyone was crazy."

"Everyone except Mink. What if he had not been there?"

"Someone else would have stopped it."

"Suppose no one had?"

"I cannot imagine it. It has been a terrible day, my grandchild. I think the worst of it is over."

I said nothing. After a time she said, "Your mother was better when I left her. She is hopeful now."

"That is good," I replied, and again we sat in silence.

"Perhaps you do not think the worst of it is over," she said.

"For today perhaps."

"But not for tomorrow?"

"I think Running By will kill him tomorrow," I said.

My grandmother hung her head and said nothing, and I was sorry I had let her know my true feelings. I looked at Two Crows sitting alone across the room. No one has much to say to a dying man. Even I had not spoken to him or looked squarely at him since it all began. Looking at him now I felt the horror coming over me again. I fought against it and worked with it until I could look at him without feeling myself losing control. Then I got up and went over and sat beside him.

For a long time neither of us spoke.

"Here we are, little one," he said quietly at last.

"Yes," I whispered.

"Do you think they will accept our offer?"

I shook my head miserably.

"Neither do I," he said, and he did not sound afraid.

"Tonight you could leave," I said. "Go down to the Lower River People."

"And then they would kill Little Buck."

"He could go with you."

"They would kill another of our brothers, or maybe an uncle. Or maybe even you. It is a Bird life they want. Mine is simply the first one of their choice."

There was no way out. "Cries Victory will be trying to help us," I said lamely.

As Two Crows pressed a hand against his face, I was sorry I had said it. "Why did it have to be his nephew?" he murmured

I could think of no reply. We sat quietly for a long time. At last I said, "It is too bad you never saw the ocean."

"I always thought there would be time. I thought there would be time for everything."

"You could have died on the war trail."

"But I never thought I would. I thought I would live to be an old man."

"We expect too much from life. Everyone expects too much."

Two Crows slowly turned and looked at me. "You are growing old beyond your years, little one."

For a while longer we sat together, thinking about things, and then I got up and ate some supper. It did not seem right to be hungry at such a time, but I was, and I ate, though only a little. Night had fallen and we still waited for Four Paws and Little Buck to return. I felt encouraged that it was taking so long; I began to believe that they were negotiating how large the payment in goods should be. Finding an empty bed, I crawled onto it, exhausted. But I did not sleep. Lying in the darkness beyond the firelight, I felt comforted by the close-ness, by the faces of my kinsmen moving in and out of the firelight.

Then, when it was late, they returned. Through the dull-ness of half-sleeping I heard them, smelled tobacco smoke as the pipe was passed around the circle. I heard the murmur of Four Paws' voice, so hushed, so defeated that the words did not reach me. But I knew them. Tears slipped across my face and dropped on the blanket beneath my head as Four Paws' voice grew stronger. He said that the beloved men had lis-tened to him and to Little Buck, and they had seen the wis-dom of their words. They asked Mink to go speak for them. Mink went to the Wolf people, and standing before them, he acknowledged that the Bird clan had taken a life from the Wolf clan and left it light in the balance, and that the balance must be restored. He agreed that it was the duty of a man to avenge his brother's death. But he told them what Little Buck had said, and he reminded them of the marriage ties between the two clans. He said it was the wish of the beloved men that no more blood be spilled, and he told them that the Bird clan was willing to give as great a wealth of goods as was necessary to dry the tears of the Wolf clan, as much as was needed to restore the balance. Then Cries Victory urged acceptance of the offer. But Running By refused. Payment in goods dries the tears of the living, he reminded them, but it means nothing to the dead. It does not avenge crying blood. The others could agree if they chose to, but he would not be bound. He was the brother, and the duty fell more to him than to the others. It was his intention to send a Bird spirit to join his brother's spirit so that those two could walk together to the Darkening Land. He reminded them that this was the only way to truly set the matter straight, the only way to settle it forever.

Two Crows was to be out on the west side of the palisade at midday. There was nothing more that could be done.

I slept and dreamed that I was a child again and that they were going to shoot my dog for digging in the cornfield. And when I awoke it was with the terrible feeling that everything was wrong. There was singing. I listened and it was Two Crows singing his death song. He was singing of the accomplishments of his life, of the battles he had seen, of the times he had bested the enemy, of the war names he had won. He sang of his generosity, of the gifts he had given, of the wealth he had handed freely to others. He sang of how men are born to die, of how the path of life leads straight to death, of how his mother had said when he was born, "It is a boy. He will fight and he will die."

I looked up through the smokehole and saw that it was morning. I stood up shakily. The house was almost empty now. Little Buck sat with Four Paws and two of my other uncles and stared in grim silence into the fire. All the women were gone, weeping together in one of my mothers' houses. I did not want to know which one. I went outside and saw Two Crows sitting alone beside the door. He was painted black from head to foot, with the symbols of his war honors fastened in his hair. He sat straight and stared ahead and sang his death song. I felt as if I did not know him.

I walked around behind our house, past the granary and on past the house of another of our kinsmen and came to the last house before the palisade. I went behind this house and sat leaning against the wall, alone, staring at the palisade a little way in front of me, seeing the valley in tiny slivers through the spaces between the timbers. The town was strangely quiet, and Two Crows' song floated over it, circling slowly like a buzzard. I felt sorrow for my mother, and for my father. I wondered if their marriage would end. There was nothing in me but sorrow. I wept, and Two Crows' song went on and on in a never ending circle.

Then it stopped. I caught my breath and listened to the silence. I heard voices, a few voices and then more. Only slowly did I realize that all was not proceeding as it should. It was not time for Two Crows to stop singing. Then it occurred to me that he had killed himself, that he had restored the balance by spilling his own blood, that he had done it himself to deny Running By the pleasure. I felt empty. Suddenly I wanted to be with the women; I wanted to cling to my mothers and sisters and cry and wail. I got to my feet and started back to my house, numb and dreamlike, and I saw people hurrying back and forth between the houses.

But they were happy! "What is it?" I cried. "What is it?"

Quail Moccasin, my mother's sister, ran to me and threw her arms around me. "He is saved, my daughter! Your brother is saved!"

"Tell me!" I stared at her, breathing hard, and she told me how Turkey Woman had been the one, how Turkey Woman had heard Two Crows singing his death song and could not bear it; how she had seen Cries Victory weeping, her own brother, and she could not bear it; how she had called together her clansmen and had spoken to them. She told them that the grief she was suffering at the death of her son was all that she could bear; that it would be a cruel thing if any son or brother of hers added to it by spilling the blood of Two Crows; that Two Crows was her own brother's son, whose name she herself had chosen at his birth; that any person who would spill his blood would be stabbing a knife into her own heart; that if any brother or son of hers should do such a thing, she would never look upon his face again, nor say his name, nor think the smallest thought of him; that it would be as if that son or brother were dead to her. Those were her words and they were more than Running By could stand against. So the Wolf clan sent a message that a payment in goods would set the matter straight.

It took almost a month to gather together enough goods to satisfy them. Every person in the Bird clan contributed what he had, and the men went into the hills to find more skins and meat, and the women wove cloth and tanned hides and made pouches and sashes and belts rich with beadwork. And when we were finished, all the people of the town gathered at the plaza and we presented the payment to the Wolf clan. We gave it to them piece by piece, showing each item around the circle, and it took most of the morning to complete it. Then Gray Hawk stood before us and said that all of the Seven Clans had seen the payment made, that the tears of the bereaved had been dried up, that the balance had been restored.

"It is over," he said. "Let us speak of it no more. The Wolf people and the Bird people are brothers and sisters once again."

But it was not over. It is wrong ever to think that a payment in goods can settle a matter of blood.

FOUR

On a spring evening, as the sun was setting, Mink came with Crazy Eyes to our house. I was sitting beside the outside fire with my parents and my grandmother, and when I saw the two of them approaching, I was surprised. But it was not Crazy Eyes I was surprised to see. Since the incident at the ball ground it was not at all unusual to look up and see my grandfather, full of age, making his way slowly into our yard, steadying his old legs with his walking stick. He would come especially to see Two Crows and Little Buck because those two no longer went near the house of Turkey Woman. It was one of the ways in which things had changed. If the matter of blood was truly settled, things should have gone on as before, with no darkness or bitter feeling. It had been more than a year since the killing, and we had been through a New Corn Festival where the hardness between people is softened and relationships renewed, where all that is old and unclean is washed away and the new year is started with nothing between us but a whiteness of heart. But in Running By's eyes the injustice had not been wiped away, and so Two Crows and Little Buck would not taunt him by going to his mother's house nor to any house of the Bird clan. It seemed clear that the matter was not truly settled but simply held in abeyance. And so Crazy Eyes came often to visit my brothers. But never before had Mink come with him.

As my mother set the food pot closer to the heat, I went into the house and brought out two cane mats and two blankets and spread them on the west side of the fire, the place of honor. When I saw my father rise stiffly to greet our guests, I went back to the house and got another blanket, and when he sat down again, I put it around his shoulders. The chill of the evening was bad for his arthritis.

Crazy Eyes smiled at me. "Rain Dove treats her father well."

"She is a good daughter," said Cries Victory.

"It is good that you both have come," my grandmother said to our guests. She handed them each a wooden bowl and moved the ladle around so that it leaned toward them against the side of the food pot.

"I told my nephew about the good food you always have here," said Crazy Eyes. "He had to come and try it for himself."

"It is good that you have come," my mother said to Mink.

Our two guests put a little of the food into their bowls and while they ate it, scooping it up with their fingers, we did not talk. They did not eat like hungry men, and I knew they had not come for the food.

"Two Crows is not here?" said Crazy Eyes.

"No," said my father. "He and Little Buck have gone over the mountain for some dried meat they cached during the winter hunt. I started out with them this morning but had to turn back."

"The arthritis," said Crazy Eyes.

"Yes. It is getting worse in my knee. Now it is there and in the shoulder."

"It pains a father to see age coming so soon to his son."

"It is not so soon, my father."

"But you are not even as old as my nephew here, and look at him—he is a young man."

I smiled because I thought my grandfather was making a joke. Mink was not a young man. His face was lined, and many of his hairs were gray, and his arms and his legs and his chest had lost much of the firmness of youth. Mink was not young, but as I looked at him and at my father, I realized that Cries Victory did indeed look older. That was something else that had changed since the killing.

"There is a curious story going around the townhouse today," said Crazy Eyes. "It has to do with a canoe. A canoe on the southern ocean. But by saying canoe, I do not exactly mean canoe. I mean a huge thing like a townhouse that floats on the water. Odder still, it has great cloths above it stretched out on poles so that they catch the wind and move the thing along. And men live on it. Spirit people, I think. Immortals."

"It doesn't always stay on the ocean," said Mink. "Sometimes it comes into the mouths of rivers, and sometimes the Immortals come ashore. They are very unusual looking."

"Perhaps they are Water Cannibals," said my grandfather. "Like those that live at the bottoms of some of our rivers."

"I don't understand how a townhouse could float," said my father.

"It is a spirit canoe," explained Crazy Eyes.

"They say it is made of split pieces of wood that are fastened together in some fashion," said Mink. "I suppose that if they could keep the water from coming in, it might float. Maybe they fill the cracks with resin."

"If it is a spirit canoe, it does not matter," said Crazy Eyes. "If the spirit people wanted a canoe made even of rock, it would just be a matter of carving it."

"How do people interpret such a story?" asked Cougar Woman.

"I do not believe it, myself," said Crazy Eyes.

"I think it is the same story we heard several years ago," said Mink. "The one about the floating townhouse and the beings with copper clothing. I think it is the same story going around again."

"Do these Immortals also eat human food?" asked my father.

"Yes, it is said that they do. Just like before. It seems to me to be the same story."

"Someone made it up for scaring children," said Cougar Woman.

"That is how it seems to me," said Crazy Eyes.

Mink said nothing, and for a time there was a silence.

"It is cool," said Day Moon. "We should move inside, and I will make some tea. I have some sassafras that we dug just today."

"Fresh sassafras," said Mink. "There is a sign of spring. And the peepers. Listen, and you can hear them singing. They are the early ones."

We sat for a time and listened to the tiny, high-pitched voices of the spring frogs, listened to the loveliness of their song. The stars were out now and it was very cool and we shivered, feeling for the heat of the fire. It gave me pleasure to have Mink in our midst, at ease in the friendliness of our circle.

My mother rose and went to build up the inside fire and start the tea. After a while the rest of us got up, Mink remembering my father's arthritis and giving him a hand to help him to his feet. I expected then that our guests would leave because Two Crows and Little Buck were not there and because they had already told us the news—the tale from the townhouse. Instead, they were inclined to visit, and they came inside with us, taking their places around the hearth.

My father passed his tobacco pouch, and for a time there was silence. Then Crazy Eyes said, "It saddens me that things have not settled between my grandsons."

"It saddens us all," said my father. "It is a hard thing. Of all that has happened in my life, this has been the hardest."

I was startled at what was being said, that they should be speaking of this thing that was never mentioned.

"There was more to be learned about people in that one day at the ball ground than in seven years of ordinary days," said Mink.

He paused and no one said anything. I was beginning to feel uncomfortable.

"People always have a pretense," he continued. "They are like masked dancers. They have wooden faces and a stylized manner that they parade before others, and they never forget themselves. Except that very rarely a day comes like that one, and all the music stops and the dancers become confused, and they think that what they are doing must not be life, it must be dreaming. So they drop their masks and forget themselves, because in a dream there is no one there to see. But I was seeing all of it and I found it to be a day of rare sights. As when the one walking near me on unsteady legs reached out without a thought and took my arm and clung to it for support. Had she not forgotten herself, she would never have done it. But she needed an arm and she took the nearest one, without the least worry of what the owner of the arm or anyone else would think of it."

There was silence, until my father said, "Do you remember it, my daughter?"

I looked away, startled that Mink might have been speaking of me. "I remember very little of that day," I said, but as I spoke I began remembering.

"I'm certain you were the one," said Mink. "I remember it clearly."

"It is possible. I think that for a short time I did hold on to someone's arm, but I never looked to see who it was."

"It was I."

I was embarrassed to think what I had done, that I had taken his arm as if he had been someone familiar, some brother or uncle, as if he were not Mink of the Deer clan, the most powerful of the priests, the seer of omens. I looked at the floor in front of me, wondering why he should want to embarrass me.

"For you it was a bad day," said Mink. "You do not like to speak of it."

"Nor even to think of it," I said.

"But there were things about it that I myself do not forget," said Mink. "Things I don't want to forget. Those rare sights should be remembered. The young woman, hardly more than a child, standing with the men in battle. That should not be forgotten."

I waited, hoping that my mother or my father would say something, that they would turn the discussion away from me. But there was only silence. What were they doing? An anger began to grow within me.

"There is nothing glorious about insanity," I said shortly. "It should be forgotten."

"So you view it as insanity."

"Very clearly. That was how I saw it then, and that is how I see it now."

"But in the end you saved your brother's life."

I looked at Mink. "Because you came forward and brought us to our senses. Otherwise we would have lost far more lives than my brother's. For that we owe you a great debt."

"You are too humble," said Mink. "Yours was an act of courage that people will not forget. I was greatly moved by it. The memory will always be with me."

I glanced around the circle in confusion. They were doing something, weaving in and out around me, wrapping me up like some helpless thing trapped in a web.

But suddenly Mink said, "It is getting late." Then he and Crazy Eyes were on their feet and my father and my mother were rising, offering to walk with them to the plaza. I watched them go, the four of them walking away from me, ducking out through the door one after the other, until all at once they were gone. I was alone with my grandmother.

In dazed silence I sat looking at the fire. Finally I said, "You had little to say tonight."

"I was listening," said Cougar Woman. "And I heard a great deal. There are things your mother has not bothered to tell me."

"Nor me. What is it that is going on?"

"You do not know?"

"Not exactly," I said, looking down at my hands. "But I am in the middle of it."

"You are in the middle of it, and Mink is in the middle of it. I think you have an idea of what it is."

"But I won't say it. I would feel very foolish, because I know it isn't true."

"Yes it is. Mink wants to marry you."

Hearing her say it, I felt a rush that was all together shock and pleasure and dismay. I clasped my hands tightly in my lap, and my face flushed hot and my eyes stung as if I were about to cry.

"Why should he want to marry me?" I whispered.

"He takes his wives from our clan. Hawk Sister is a Bird, and so was the other wife, the one who died."

"But there are others he could choose."

"There are always others, but you are the one he has noticed. And I think your grandfather has been encouraging him."

"Crazy Eyes?"

"Yes, and Crazy Eyes has told your father about it, and your father has told your mother, and now they are all doing what they can to make it happen."

"And you?"

"I am going to do everything I can to stop it."

"You don't like Mink."

"I do not care to see my grandchild marry an old man."

"He's not that old."

"Yes he is. Compared to Trapper and Blue Shoes, he is very old indeed. Older even than your father. He has a wife who is old enough to be your mother. You would be the little wife—her slave and his plaything. And do not think there would be so much playing, either. He is an old man, do not forget, and most nights when he goes to bed, he is looking for sleep and nothing more. You are young and you should have a young man to take you for his first wife and build a house for you near your mother, a house where you will be in charge, where you alone will welcome him home. You should have a young man who can show you what the night is made for. I do not want to see you marry Mink."

"Why do the others want it?"

"There is a saying that the young man courts the woman, but the old man courts her parents."

"They know he is an important man," I said. "I felt honored to have him at our fire."

"There is prestige, and there is happiness. But often they are not the same."

I waved my hands, wishing it all away. "How can we talk like this when we are not even sure what is really happening?"

"I am sure," said Cougar Woman. "I have eyes and I have ears, and I am sure."

I tossed that night, barely sleeping. But when I awoke it was late in the morning, and only my mother was there.

"Where is everyone?" I asked.

"Someone started games at the plaza."

"You did not want to go?"

"No, my daughter. I wanted to talk to you."

"To tell me that Mink wants to marry me."

"Yes, to tell you that."

For a long time neither of us said anything more. My mother seemed to be busy sewing, but I knew she was not thinking about her work. At last she said, "It is an honor."

"But I may choose not to accept it."

"You may choose as you wish, but it is still an honor."

"How would you choose, my mother, if it were you?"

"I would consider every aspect of it very carefully, though perhaps I would think a little too much about the honor of it, and about the comforts a man in his position could provide."

"Would you think about whether you could feel tenderly for such a man?"

"Yes, and I think that I could care for him. He is very kind."

"But you are not so far from him in age."

"That is true. From where I am, he seems very kind. But it is your choice."

"He is powerful."

"More than any man in the town. More than Gray Hawk, who is headman. It would be a great honor to be his wife. You would be treated with a respect such as I myself have never known. You would be the wife of Mink."

"One of his wives," I said.

"Hawk Sister is a good person. She would make a splendid co-wife."

"And treat me like a slave."

"No woman has to stay in a marriage if she is unhappy. Co-wives often love each other like sisters. Crazy Eyes has said that it is Hawk Sister who has asked Mink to find another wife to take the place of the one who died. It seems she misses the companionship."

"She is a little old to be my sister."

"If you are married to the same man, you will feel like sisters."

"Have you invited him to make the formal visit to have my answer?"

"I must talk first to my brothers. They will want to know how you feel about it."

"I don't know how I feel. I need to talk to my grandmother some more."

"Talk also to your grandfather. Mink is his clan nephew, and he knows him well."

"I will talk to both of them."

My mother busied herself with her sewing as I stared into the fire.

"You must be hungry," she said at last. "The food is by the outside fire."

"I am not sure I can eat. All of this is happening too quickly. I don't even know Mink."

"You will feel better if you eat a little," said my mother.

The trees were in full leaf, spring turning to summer, when Hawk Sister, the wife of Mink, came to visit. I was sitting in the yard making pottery when she arrived, and I did not see her come. I heard my mother say, "She is there," and looked up and saw her walking toward me. She seemed a pleasant woman, near the age of my mother, with a broad face and handsome, gentle eyes. She wore shell around her neck and arms, and her skirt was white mulberry cloth.

"It is good that you have come—" I hesitated, not knowing how to address her.

"It is good to be here, my younger sister." Not child, but sister.

There was an empty mat beside me, and I reached over nervously brushed it off with my hand. "Perhaps it is a little dirty," I said.

"No, it is fine." As she sat beside me, perspiration trickled beneath my arms. My fingers suddenly felt clumsy, and I put down the clay and clasped my hands together in my lap. We sat in silence. I struggled to calm myself, to keep my head clear and in control.

"Your pottery is very nice," said Hawk Sister.

"It is something I enjoy," I said.

There was another silence and I began to sense that she too was nervous. This woman who was older and so highly regarded, sitting here in the yard of this ordinary family, away from the plaza, away from power and influence, she extraordinary and I ordinary—the distance between us narrowed when I sensed that she too was nervous.

"It feels like summer today," I said. "I suppose there will soon be war parties going out."

"Will your brothers be going?"

"Little Buck, yes, but not Two Crows. Not soon, anyway. He is to be married on the new of the moon."

"To Rising Moon, I believe."

"Yes. To Rising Moon."

"She will make a good wife," said Hawk Sister. "She has waited a long time for your brother."

I smiled. "He could think only of war honors. She must care for him a great deal to have waited."

"I suppose you will miss him when he moves to her house."

"I don't see him so much anymore as it is. But I'm sure he will come often to visit. A man needs his kinsmen."

"Rising Moon does not live so far from my house," said Hawk Sister. "I see her often. She passes on her way to the plaza. Sometimes with Two Crows. I suppose when they are married, I will see much more of him."

She paused, and I said nothing.

"You could live there too," she said. For a moment she seemed flustered, but then she steadied. "My husband wants another wife. I want him to have another wife. I want a companion, a sister to take the place of the one who died. Mink tells me that you are the one he would choose."

"And why would he choose me?" I felt suddenly that she was someone to whom I could speak earnestly. "I am so young and insignificant."

"He thinks you are fresh as sunlight and spirited and intelligent and greatly significant."

"But he does not know me."

"He feels that he knows you very well. He has watched you and noticed much about you."

"But I don't know him."

"You have grown up in this town. You have seen much of him."

"But perhaps I have not noticed so much."

"Well then, I can tell you about him. What would you like to know? I can tell you that he snores." She laughed.

"Tell me what he would be like as my husband."

"He would be kind, but also very busy. He is often gone before dawn to attend to some curing or ceremony. He spends most evenings with the beloved men working out the problems of the town. And the time that is free, that he should spend with us, he uses to go walking alone, thinking, pondering things I cannot even imagine. But when we do get to see him, when he comes home to eat or to go to bed at night, then we find him kind and thoughtful and we feel very fortunate to be married to him."

"You speak as if I already were."

"I wish you were. I hope you will say yes when it is time. My house is lonely without a co-wife." She paused and then she said, "And I will tell you truly that I also need someone to share the work. With Mink, there is not so much to do as in other households because he is given many things for his services, things that we then do not have to make. But there are often guests to entertain, so there is a great deal of cooking and such as that. And now I am speaking truly and frankly. I am telling you beforehand that often I do not feel well; often there is something inside me that attacks and causes discomfort and makes me very tired. No one has been able to cure it, and I suppose I will someday die with it. But as for now, I need someone to be there to take over and manage things when I am not well. Sometimes one or another of my sisters comes, but they all have families of their own and it is not right to call on them too much. I need a co-wife because I need help, and I am speaking frankly to you about this because you should know. But I promise that in every way we will share the work. If I can only do a little when I am sick, then you will only do a little when I am well. I would like for you to come, my younger sister. I think our house would be a happier place."

"And do you think I would be happier there than with a young warrior in a house built for me near my mother?"

"Mink would care for you and show you tenderness and affection. But how can I say where you would be happier? Who can say that for anyone?"

"You have been open with me, and I am grateful. I am going to consider it carefully, but I cannot say that I will choose to marry him."

"I ask only that you consider it. But now I must leave, my little sister. There are guests tonight."

"I hope you are feeling well enough to prepare for them."

"Yes. Today I am very well. Today I will manage beautifully." She smiled, and in her eyes there was a friendliness that seemed genuine.

"I will consider it all carefully," I said again as she rose.

"Please do. Mink likes you very much."

As I watched her walk away, I noticed the string of shell beads woven into the black knot of her hair. I had not had so much as a single strand of shell to wear around my neck since we had given away so many of our possessions for Two Crows' life.

"There is also the matter of Two Crows," said Crazy Eyes.

"How do you mean?" I asked. We were speaking softly so that Turkey Woman, pounding corn outside, could not hear us.

"I live here where I see a great deal of Running By. Not so

· 60 ·

much as before he married, but still he comes often to sit with us, and I know him; I know much about him. His heart is bitter against Two Crows. For him the matter is not settled. But Turkey Woman stands firm in her love for your father and your brother—though she never sees Two Crows anymore, which is too bad because every day he owes his life to her. If she were gone, Running By would not wait a day to hide himself along some trail where Two Crows would be coming and put an arrow through his heart. But of this I am not worried at the moment because Turkey Woman will not have it. What worries me is that Running By will resort to more subtle means, that he will hire a conjurer. And this is where the matter of Two Crows touches upon the matter of Mink."

"Running By would hire Mink?"

"No. He would never hire Mink. I think he would have to go beyond the town to find someone to hire. But Mink, you see, could be Two Crows' protection. There would be far more danger in going against the brother-in-law of Mink than there would be in going against Two Crows as he is now. Much more danger. Conjury turned back strikes down the sender, you know."

"Did Mink speak to you of this?" I said.

"Yes, but it was something I was already thinking of."

"And I suppose my mother and my father have it in mind as well."

"We all do. You ask me why I think you should marry Mink and I tell you all of it. Your mother is a kinder person than I. She seeks to spare you this pressure on your choosing. But I see you as a young woman full of intelligence who should know everything the rest of us are thinking in this matter. Or perhaps it is just that I love Two Crows too much."

"And so you put on me the pressure that my mother in her kindness spared me?"

"Yes. I cannot help myself."

"But my mother sent me to you. She wanted me especially to talk to you. So, you see, in her kindness she also loves Two Crows, but not too much, nor do you, nor do I. We all love him because he deserves it, and I'm glad to know all of this. It wouldn't be right to choose without knowing the choices. But I also love myself. When I decide, it will be after considering everything, not just this."

"This is as it should be, my beloved grandchild. Do not think that I lack concern for your happiness. I know you and I know Mink, and it is my true feeling that you two would get along together. You are not ordinary. I think you would do well as Mink's wife in that house beside the plaza, living in the center of things. He is a man of great intellect and deep understanding, and there is much you can learn from him, much he will tell you if he knows that you are listening. . . . I care very much for Two Crows, my grandchild, but I also care for you."

"And I for you, my grandfather. Very much."

I had talked to everyone about marrying Mink except Mink himself. Since the evening of his first visit, he had not returned. Spring had blossomed and gone, and summer had come with its fields of corn, beans, squash, and sunflowers— fields that had to be hoed and hilled with the sun beating down. I had time to think in the fields, and some days I would decide, yes, and other days, no, and always I said to myself, If I could just talk to him again, if only I could look at him and listen to him and imagine how it would be.

Then one day in midsummer my mother told me that Mink had been to talk to my uncles, that they had invited him to come for the formal visit.

"When he comes, you will have to give your answer," she said. "I would approve a betrothal, and my sisters and my brothers would approve, and your brothers would, although Two Crows is not altogether enthusiastic. You will prepare the corn mush for Mink's visit, but whether or not you let him eat it is your own choice. We cannot decide for you."

"When is it to be?"

"In four days."

"I think I'll be glad to finally decide it one way or the other," I said. "This has been a difficult time."

"And a little exciting?" my mother said, gently teasing.

"More than a little," I laughed.

I thought that deciding would be easy, that it would soon be over and I would be free again. I wished for that. But it was not so easy, and suddenly there was only one day left before the visit. I went to the fields as usual, trying to appear decisive and in control. But soon I could stand the work no longer. I left and walked into the town, wandering toward the plaza, steering toward the place where Hawk Sister's house stood, where she and Mink lived together. I wanted to see them at home in their yard, to feel how it would be to live there. But at the last moment I was afraid of being noticed and averted my eyes, walking past them without looking, pre-tending to be busy on some errand, going along as if I were unaware that I was there.

Out of sight, I stopped and stood for a moment, wondering what to do. Then I turned back, going more slowly now, stealthily, looking for a place from which to watch. I chose the granary of the neighboring house, and for the rest of the day I stood beside it, sometimes drawing back into the shadows, but always peering out again, watching Hawk Sister in her yard—and watching Mink. It was awesome to see the people who associated with him: Gray Hawk and all the beloved men, a constant coming and going. And near the end of the day I saw two visitors from the Lower River come to Mink's fire, important men in fine clothing, decked with feathers and ornaments. For a long time I watched and tried to feel how it would be. But in the end I could not imagine that important place as my house, nor Mink as my husband. At dusk I left and walked slowly home, feeling a sadness.

Only my grandmother was not outside in our yard. My family stopped speaking as I approached, but I passed by them in silence and went into the house. Outdoors it had been twilight, but here there was no fire and it was dark.

"My grandmother?" I said softly.

"I am here," she said. "Come sit with me."

I could see her now, barely, and I went and sat beside her in the cool darkness. My shoulders drooped and I sat without thought, feeling only the aching in the center of my soul.

"I have decided," I said at last. "I'll not let him eat the corn mush."

For a moment there was silence. Then she said, "I am relieved to hear it, my grandchild. But I think it makes you sad."

"A little. Perhaps after tomorrow I will go stay awhile with our kinsmen at Bear Hill. Maybe I can find something there to cheer me."

"I would like to see you do that. You have decided well. I will be happy to see you marry some fine young warrior."

I said nothing.

"Come on," she said. "Let's go see what there is to eat."

"You go, my grandmother. I think I would like to stay in here. I think maybe I will go to sleep."

"I will bring you something."

"No. Please don't bother. I'm not hungry. I just want to go to sleep."

My chin trembled and I was glad it was too dark for her to see. I wanted her to leave, and when she did, I got up and went to my bed and crawled on it with tears slipping down my face. I drew up a blanket, not because I was cold but because I needed the comfort of being covered and alone in the dark. Then I wept with a loneliness that reached deep into the center of my soul.

I awoke before dawn. The others were still sleeping as I sat on the edge of my bed and stared out into the darkness beyond the doorway. I dreaded the day. I dreaded having Mink come and having to refuse his offer of marriage.

In the faint dawn a mockingbird began to sing, and I got up alone and went out to start the fire in the cookshed. As the others awoke, I cooked breakfast for them and ate hungrily myself, not having eaten the night before. The sun was above the trees before my mother mentioned the corn mush. She wondered how soon I should start it.

"There's no hurry," I said. "I don't want it to be ready when he is here."

Day Moon said nothing, but I knew she was disappointed. They all would be disappointed. All except Cougar Woman. And maybe Two Crows. It was hard to know what he must be feeling. On the one hand he did not want me to marry just to protect him from conjury; and yet who is there who would not like to have his life protected? But I had worked that out in my mind. Mink could be hired as well as married, and that was the way we would deal with it. Every so often we could hire him to do a divination at the river to find out whether anyone was conjuring against Two Crows. It would cost something, but I myself was willing never to wear another piece of shell if that was what was necessary.

The sun moved higher, until I could not put off the corn mush any longer. So I began, draining the lye water from the corn my mother had left soaking overnight. I put the swollen kernels in a basket and went down to the river to rinse them. Then I came home and pounded the corn in the mortar and then flipped it in a fan basket to let the hulls blow away. Then I sifted it, put the large pieces back in the mortar and pounded some more, sifted, and pounded one more time. Then I put it all in a pot of water I had boiling on the fire, moved it from the center of the heat, put in a wooden spoon for stirring, and left it there to simmer.

I went inside and took from the basket beneath my bed my white mulberry cloth skirt, the one I saved for dances and festivals, and I put it on. I took down my hair and rubbed it with bear oil scented with spicebush. My grandmother combed it for me and fastened it up again. I had no shell, but I put bone ear pins through my earlobes and tied a string of long wooden beads, carved and painted, around my neck.

"There," I said. "I am ready."

"You look lovely," said Cougar Woman. She was the only one who felt like talking.

Four Paws came, and Two Crows; my father left because a formal visit was a clan affair, and he would have felt out of place. Little Buck was there, and my mother and my grandmother, and we all waited around the fire in the shade of the cookshed and said very little to each other, until at last our guest arrived.

Mink looked very striking on that day. He wore a cape of feathers, white feathers of the snowy egret. He wore ear spools that were covered with engraved copper, and at his neck there was a round shell pendant with a sprightly dancer engraved upon it. And in his hair Mink wore the skin of a dove, a gray-white dove, lovely and lifelike with wings spread. When I saw it, I blushed, feeling he was wearing it for me, because my name meant a dove calling after the summer rain.

Mink sat down at the place that was spread for him on the west side of the circle, and Four Paws greeted him, saying, "It is good that you have come."

"It is very good to be here," said Mink, carefully avoiding any terms of relation. We were not his real kinsmen and under the circumstances it would have been quite improper to speak as if we were.

In the silence that followed, I tried to still the trembling nervousness that had taken hold of me on his arrival. I was too aware of how closely we had to sit, he on the west side of the fire and I next to him on the north. On the eastern side beside me was Four Paws, my uncle, and in a line beside him were my mother, Two Crows, and Little Buck, and finally, on the south, my grandmother. Mink was the first to speak.

"I had been hoping for a summer rain before I came."

"It would have been most appropriate," said Four Paws with a smile. I was embarrassed to be the center of attention, and I looked down at my hands.

"I don't think we'll see rain today," said Two Crows, glancing at the sky. We all peered skyward, nodding in agreement.

"It's unfortunate," said Mink. "The corn has been too long without it. I was just speaking to Gray Hawk about the need for a ceremony. Two men from Lower River are visiting, and it seems it has been even drier down there. It's worse for them because their corn is ahead of ours and is at the point of making ears—the crucial time for water. They've had ceremonies which have failed, and the priests are blaming the people for unrighteous living and the people are blaming the priests for weakness in power. Just the sort of thing we don't want to see here."

"Do you think there is a danger?" said Four Paws.

"There is always a danger that things will go wrong—that the priests will not read the signs correctly, that the ceremonies will not be started in time, that they will be ineffective because of the transgressions of the people."

"And at this time of year the danger is worse," I said, finding myself speaking easily, the nervousness gone from me.

A smile passed over Mink's face, not a smile that moved the corners of his mouth, but one that seemed to come from somewhere around his eyes. "Yes," he said, "this time of year does make it worse. The last month before the New Corn Festival is the very time we need most to have rain, the very time we need most to have our ceremonies work if we have to use them, and yet it is the very time of the year that is farthest from the renewal and purification of the last Festival of the New Corn. We are most in need of purity at the very time the most pollution has accumulated in our lives. We are in need of purity, and yet we cannot have it without renewal. Yet we cannot have renewal without new corn. And we cannot have new corn without rain, and we cannot have rain without purity."

"We walk in a circle, never coming to the end," I said. "There is no way to stop and start over with a slightly better order of things."

There was a pause, and I stole a glance at Mink and saw

the smile passing again across his face. "I would like to steal a taste of that corn mush," he said. My heart jumped and for a moment I froze. Then I leaned forward, hesitating, but I reached the spoon before he did. Trembling, I took it and began to stir.

"N-no," I stammered. "It isn't . . . it's not ready yet."

"That's too bad," said Mink. "It smells so good. Perhaps I'll have a chance to taste it later."

"I don't know," I said uncertainly. "It cooks very slowly."

"That was a black circle you painted for the corn," said Two Crows, and I loved my brother for stepping in to help me. "One wonders how it is that we ever make a crop."

Mink laughed. "Perhaps because we are not totally corrupt. Usually the rains come. There are few summers when drought threatens, and fewer still when our priests fail to bring back the rain. Perhaps we can thank the First People for choosing to live in these mountains. It rains more in the mountains than anywhere else. The Lower River People have far more droughts than we. Either they are more corrupt, or their First People chose a worse place for them to live."

"Perhaps it is a little of both," said Cougar Woman, and we all chuckled.

"I don't suppose they are inviting us to their festival this year," said Two Crows.

"They are inviting us, but it wouldn't be kind to go. I doubt they will have enough corn for themselves."

"And this was the year I had planned to go," said Two Crows. "I wanted to take my new wife to see the ocean. Every year I have wanted to go see the ocean, and this year I was going to do it."

"Then you should go anyway," said Mink. "Never mind

the festival. The ocean alone is worth the trip. It's not really so far. It will take you six days to reach Big Town on the Lower River. You can stop there and rest, and then it's two more days down the river to the ocean. You will find the ocean something beyond imagining. The beauty of it cannot be described. There is water as far as you can see, stretching out to the edge of the dome of the sky. Blue and green water, flecked with white that is the tops of the waves, and the waves can be seen far out in the distance. But near the shore they are larger. Near the shore they rise up in great size, foaming white like our rapids, but not at all like rapids. They heave up in a great curl and roll in toward the shore and crash down, one after another, with a thundering sound that never ceases. But the sound is not really like thunder. It is more like great rapids, or like a waterfall—yet not so continuous as that. More like a heavy wind in the trees that rises and falls. And always at the ocean there is the sound of the white birds that live by fishing, birds that are always swooping and turning across the water and up against the sky with a cry that is like a loud creaking, a continuous creaking above the sound of the waves. And the shore itself is a thing of great beauty, especially where there is sand, white sand without any other soil. The waves, after each one has crashed, run up onto the sand, each one separately, running up shallow and harmless, coming just so far and then stopping and running back again with a pull that you can see, that you can feel with your feet if you are standing in it. The sand is strewn with shells, every kind of shell you can imagine. And there are pieces of wood that are worn smooth and bleached white by the water and the sun, wood that has come from some other part of the shore and has been washed up and scattered among the shells. And there are dead weeds on the sand, several kinds of weeds that come from the ocean. And there is always a wind blowing in from the water, and the trees near the shore are like those on a high mountaintop, small and twisted and shaped round by the wind. . . . You should see it for yourself. The beauty is more than I can ever describe. If you have never been there, you should go."

"Only eight days away," said Two Crows. "The way you speak of it, I wish I could leave today."

"Wait a few days and go back with the two who are visiting. I'll speak to them and they'll be happy to have you along. You and your wife. They will provide you with a boat and a guide to take you from their town to the ocean."

"Perhaps they wouldn't mind having three along," said Little Buck.

"You are welcome to come," said Two Crows. "You can do the paddling. You and Rising Moon. I'll just lie back and watch the clouds."

All was relaxed and friendly now. I sat at ease and listened to Mink and marveled at the depth of his knowledge. As the day continued, I sometimes spoke, and when I did, that smile would pass across his face—I would always see it when I looked. But mostly it was he who spoke, and through the morning and into the afternoon I listened to him, feeling very comfortable and easy beside him. At dusk he was still there and we were tired and hungry from talking all day and not eating, and it was then that Mink looked at me and smiled and said, "Surely that corn mush is ready now."

I did not look at him when he said it. I looked at the corn mush in the pot. It was dry and caked from sitting too long by the fire. I reached out and took the spoon and tried to stir it, but it had scorched and was stuck to the sides of the pot. I began to laugh. It was such a mess that I could not help myself, and laughing I took the spoon from the pot and handed it to him and said, "Such as it is, it is ready."

He was smiling, but trying not to, and he dipped the spoon into the pot and managed to get out a piece of the dried mush. He ate it. "Very good," he said. "Rather chewy." Then his shoulders began to tremble and he was laughing too, both of us laughing, I behind my hands, shaken at what I had done.

FIVE

Mink's clan gave a wedding feast. It took place in the plaza, a public affair, and there were games from morning until night and dancing that lasted until dawn. But though it was given in my honor, I did not enjoy it very much. For me it was the beginning of something unknown, the door to a life unfamiliar, and inside myself, in my heart, I was bewildered and afraid. Had it not been that the feast was in my honor, I would have left long before it ended. When the dawn finally came and the dancing was over, I was exhausted. I wished very much to return to my mother's house. But now I was the wife of Mink, and I walked beside him to the house of Hawk Sister. She had gone ahead of us, and when we arrived, she hugged me and said, "Here you are at your house. It belongs to the two of us now."

I smiled and said nothing.

"In time you will feel it is your own," said Mink.

"I am sure I will," I said. But in my heart I did not believe it. I was uncertain of myself and ill at ease.

"Your brothers brought your things, and I put them there," said Hawk Sister, pointing to a little nook against the wall, a nook screened by cane mats hanging from the ceiling. "That bed will be yours."

I wanted to go at once and fall into it, but I was Mink's new wife, and I did not know what he expected of me. I was afraid he would want to follow me to my bed, and I was nervous about that and felt too weary to deal with it. So I sat down uncertainly by the fire, and without intending to, I gave a sigh.

"You need to sleep," Mink said gently. "Try not to worry about things, little wren. You'll like it here when you get used to it. You had a tiring night. You should go to your bed now and try to sleep a while."

Without him, he seemed to be saying, and I felt a measure of relief. I got up and went to my new bed, my place of privacy behind the hanging mats. I undressed and slipped beneath a cover of deerskin, soft and light and luxurious. I lay there in that strange place, uncertain that I would be able to sleep in the morning light. And my heart beat fast and loud until I was certain that Mink would not follow me, until I heard him go to another bed and lie down upon it, until I heard the soft sound of his snoring. I looked around and thought to myself, This morning it is strange and new, but in time it will be a familiar place, even comforting—not now, perhaps, but in time. *Little wren.* I liked it when he called me little wren.

I slept. When I awoke it was night and I was lost. Then slowly, very slowly, I remembered that I was married, that I was Mink's wife, that I was in my new house, in my new bed. I sat up and put my feet on the floor and reached out in the darkness and touched one of the cane mats. It was real; this was my life; this change had truly taken place. I wondered if it was late in the night. I felt strange to have slept through an entire day. What was I to do now, in this unfamiliar place, in the darkness, in the middle of the night? I thought I would like to get up and go outside, but I did not know my way through the darkness here, and outside the dogs would bark at me as at a stranger. So I lay back on my bed and stared into the darkness, thinking, dozing, waiting for the light of dawn.

Hawk Sister rose with the first sign of morning, and I got up and dressed and went outside to the cookshed to help her. In the gray dawn, with the stars leaving the sky, the morning fire in the cookshed had a comforting familiarity.

"You slept a long time." Hawk Sister smiled.

"I didn't know how tired I was. I feel much better now." I stood and looked around at my new place, at the dimly lit yard, at the houses of the neighbors, at the plaza beside us with its dark townhouse. "I should get to know the dogs today," I said. "I wouldn't like to come out at night and have them bark at me."

"They will love anyone who feeds them. We have only the two—Mink does so little hunting."

I watched the morning sky growing lighter with the first red streaks of sunrise. "It feels peculiar to have missed a day. Did anything happen yesterday? Did visitors come?"

"I asked Mink not to bring anyone until you have had a chance to get used to it here."

"I don't think it will be hard," I said. But that was in the morning. Things always seem better in the morning. As the afternoon came and then the evening, a loneliness entered my heart and grew, a lost feeling, a sadness. I began to wish that I was not a second wife, that I could have had a house of my own built near my mother's, that I could have married without making such a change in things. Though I tried to hide my unhappiness, Mink and Hawk Sister saw it, and they did what they could to cheer me. Yet nothing seemed to help. At the end of the evening I crawled into my bed and stared miserably at the smokehole until I fell asleep. Mink did not come to my bed that night.

The next day was much the same except that I was beginning to learn the routine of things and I was more helpful to Hawk Sister. I tried very hard to feel content, but that is not something that can be forced.

"Tomorrow you should go visit your mother," Mink suggested in the evening.

"I will go soon," I said, "but not yet. I want to be accustomed to my new home before I go."

"Is it starting to seem better?"

"A little," I said. "I don't understand my sadness. There's nothing here to be sad about."

"We walk a path of constant changing," Mink said. "With each change there is a sadness for what we have lost and a confusion about what we have become. It happens to us again and again, and each time we are caught by surprise and do not recognize at first what has happened, because always we think we have already changed for the last time. But there is no last time."

I said nothing. But when I went to bed that night, I was not so melancholy. I lay for a long time, apprehensive, thinking that surely this would be the night Mink would come to me. I had never been a wife before. I had been a lover and had spent nights with Trapper in the corncrib. But Mink's courtship had been strange. He had never come to me that way. Now I was ashamed that I had so little experience to bring, that Trapper was the only man with whom I had ever passed the night. Perhaps I should have had more experience before I married. But it was too late for that. I had a husband now, and there would be no more nights in the corncrib. I lay in my bed, in my own house, waiting for my husband. But he did not come, and at last I fell asleep.

When I arose the next morning, Mink was gone. "Where is he?" I asked Hawk Sister.

"He left early," she said. "He didn't say where he was going. Perhaps there is a curing."

I went over to the woodpile and took up some sticks for the fire, breaking them to the right length. Kneeling by the fire and feeding the wood into it, I said, "He does not come to my bed."

"It's because you are still unhappy here," said Hawk Sister. "He thinks it best to wait."

"He has been kind to do that," I said, "but now I think it is causing me too much anxiety—because I'm not sure how it will be. I think perhaps he should come. And besides, my older sister, I'm not so unhappy anymore."

"I will speak to him," she said.

That night my husband slept with me in my bed behind the cane mats. I found it to be very much like the corncrib, except that it was more comfortable—and also he did not have to leave before the dawn, which I decided was one of the true advantages of marriage.

If there was any sadness lingering in me, it vanished the next day when Mink brought Two Crows home to visit. It had been only a few days since the feast, but I was as happy to see my brother as if we had been separated for months. And when he sat at the fire in the yard and ate from the food pot, I was proud and pleased with my new home, a place at last that was my own, a place where my brothers could come and sit and relax and be uncles to my children.

The activity at the house returned to what it had been before I came. Hardly a day went by without Gray Hawk and the beloved men seated around our fire. My only rest from it was during my times of blood when I went to the isolation of the women's house of my clan. Before I had married I had always been sorry to leave the women's house and return to my duties; but now I was finding myself anxious for my time to be over, anxious to return to the excitement of my house by the plaza. And when Hawk Sister had to stay in the women's house or when she was too ill to manage for our guests, I carried on alone and enjoyed it even more because then I did not have to leave the men after giving them their food or their tea. Hawk Sister was not interested in the things of which they spoke, and she did not expect me to be; but when she was not there, I sat near Mink, a little behind him, and listened to their words, and gradually I came to understand the workings of the town and to know the men who were at the center of things.

One night I asked Mink, as we lay together in my bed, "Do they care that I am always there listening?"

"They know whose house it is," he said. "They know they cannot send you away."

"But they would like to."

"A few, perhaps, but they have no reason. They are the ones who think women are always dangerous, in their time of blood or not. They are very stupid that way. If they don't like to find you in your own house, they can stay away. No one makes them come."

"Red Frog is one who doesn't like me."

"How do you know that, little wren?"

"I can tell."

"And who else doesn't?"

"Bender."

"Who else?"

"Big Squirrel pretends to like me, but I don't think he does."

"Why do you think he pretends?"

"Because of you. Because he values your favor. I see it in everything about him. I do not trust him very much."

Mink was silent.

"What do you think?" I said.

"I think you are an amazing little wren. I agree with you on everything." He put his arm around me and pulled me close to him and we drifted into sleep.

The next day, late in the afternoon, while I was pounding corn to make bread for the evening, Mink came alone from the townhouse and said to me, "I'm going out to walk in the valley."

"There will be fresh bread when you return," I said.

"Perhaps it would please you to walk with me."

I smiled. "It would please me, my husband, but it would not bake the bread."

Hawk Sister came out of the house then. "You should go," she said. "I'll finish the bread."

"You should be resting," I replied.

"I'm much better now. I feel like getting up and doing things. I'll finish the bread, my little sister. The two of you should walk together." I looked at Hawk Sister and felt a twinge of sorrow for her, for the ill health that returned to her in an endless circle, for the way our husband increasingly sought my company over hers.

"If you think I should go," I said.

She reached out gently for the wooden pestle.

So I left my work and went with Mink into the valley. It was in the cold season, before the first snow. All the trees were standing bare, and the land was brown. The sun was toward the west, and a chill was growing in the air. But beneath my cloak of muskrat fur I was warm. I knew as we walked through the brown cornfields toward the river that every day Mink came this way in solitude, alone with himself. I felt myself an intruder and did not speak. I wondered why he had asked me to come. We reached the river and turned upstream, walking along beneath the trees until the valley narrowed and the river trail led us into the northern hills. Beyond we could see the high mountains standing gray against the sky. We came soon to a certain stream that fed into the river, and Mink turned and followed up along it until we reached a tiny cove set into the craggy wall of a bluff that rose beside the stream. The floor of the cove was covered with last summer's ferns. There were boulders scattered about, and a great black log, moss-covered, slowly rotting upon the earth.

"Is this where you always come?" I asked.

"Not always," said Mink. "There are other places. But this one is the best."

"You're not afraid to wander out here alone?"

"Only in the summer is it very dangerous. I'm careful then, and sometimes, if there is trouble in the air, I stay in the village."

We sat on the log and for a long time we were silent, enjoying the beauty of the place. At last Mink said, "So you know the hearts of the beloved men."

"I am beginning to learn a little about them," I said. "I was surprised to find how much they are like ordinary people. They talk about different things, but even that is something they do only part of the time."

"Some of them are quite foolish," said Mink. "Not all of them, of course. Crazy Eyes is wonderfully wise, and Gray Hawk is a good man. And some of the others are deep, some of them thinkers. Without these, the town could not get along. But the stupid ones! They can never understand that we must go one way rather than the other. They look always at the small things and never see what is deep. It is something I have to deal with every day, a constant struggle to cut away an entire forest so that the dimly sighted can see the path. I have been doing it for a long time. I'm getting weary of it."

"What can they do that is so bad?"

"I will tell you the worst. Do you remember the day the Fire went out?"

"I remember a little."

"Do you remember the man who was the Keeper of the Fire that day? The man called Shaker?"

"Yes."

"And how he later killed himself?"

I nodded.

"That never should have happened," said Mink. "Shaker was completely blameless. Yet there were some who could not see it at all. They are the foolish people who do not see clearly. They do not see that everything we know is in a circle. Truth is a circle, and like any circle, there are different ways to look at it. But there is only one way that is correct. You can look at one side of a circle or another, and you will see only a part of something. If you look at all four sides, you will see all the parts. But what use is it to see all the parts if you do not know the essence of the whole? The essence of any circle is its center, and to see the truth you must look deep, you must find the center and view all the parts from there. You must bring it all together into the center of your understanding. Yet there are many who never learn this. They are the ones who would blame Shaker for an event over which he had no control. In time we persuaded them, you see, but by then it was too late to wipe away the man's humiliation. It was a senseless tragedy, and even worse because the stupid fools learned nothing from it."

"Are you always so disgusted with people?"

Mink looked at me and smiled. "Only when I'm tired. I am finding it helps to have a wren to talk to. Do you know what I mean about the center?"

"I think so," I said.

"I think you do," he said. "I felt you would."

We talked on, sitting close against the cold, lingering until the evening shadows filled the cove. Walking home, he seemed as reclutant as I to hurry, and when we were near the palisade, he said, "Will you walk with me again tomorrow?"

"I would like to," I said. "But it depends on Hawk Sister. I don't like to leave her when she's not well."

"No. I would not want you to."

"What is it that makes her ill?"

"I'm not sure what it is. It's out of my reach, you see, being her husband. Her brothers have hired good priests, but none have diagnosed it correctly."

"If you were not married to her, would you be able to cure her?"

"Perhaps not. Some very skilled curers have failed."

"There must be someone who could do something. She thinks she's going to die with it."

"So do I, little wren. In time. But I try not to think about it."

Summer returned in the circle of time, and there came a morning, a late morning, when Mink was sitting with me in the cookshed. He was drinking tea and watching me weave on the finger loom, watching me make a sash for Hawk Sister, a lovely beaded sash that I had been working on with great care for a long time. There was a serenity between us, an occasional word and long, comfortable silences. I have always kept the memory of that morning in my heart, that part of the morning, not because it was unusual in itself, but because it was the last time I was ever entirely happy. It ended when Hawk Sister hurried home from the plaza, when I saw the distress in her face.

"You must go to Gray Hawk's," she said to Mink. "Something has happened near the Lower River."

"Someone has come from there?"

"There are two, and they have a terrible story to tell, a terrible story, my husband. Gray Hawk needs you. He wonders why you are not already there."

"Because I am here," Mink said gruffly.

"Yes, and he wonders about it."

"Then let him," said Mink. He was angry and upset as he got up and hurried away to Gray Hawk's house in the plaza.

Watching him go, Hawk Sister said quietly, "They say he is spending too much time with you, my little sister. They say Rain Dove is weakening his power."

"Why should they say that? Because I'm a woman? I've never gone near him in my time of blood."

"There is a balance to be kept between a man and a woman. There is a balance and they say he's not keeping it. It's what they say, my little sister. I do not say it."

I looked down and was silent for a moment, and then I said, "There is also a balance between wives, and he does not keep that very well either."

"You mustn't think so," she said. "I am content with him. Mink and I have been together a long time, and our understanding is very deep. But between the two of you there is something different, something I could never have had with him. It pleases me that he has you for his wife. It is truly not I who feels unhappy, my little sister. It is the men. But Mink will work it out."

"What is the news?" I suddenly remembered. "What is this story they are telling?"

"Oh," groaned Hawk Sister, remembering, putting her hands to her face as she sat down beside me. "Oh, what a terrible story! What a horrible, horrible thing!"

"Tell me, my older sister."

"I was with Gray Hawk's wives and we heard it the first time it was told. I can tell it to you exactly. It happened at the ocean. The Chicoras, who live near the Lower River People, those of the Chicoras who live closest to the ocean, they are the ones it happened to." Hawk Sister paused and looked at me. "These are not the same words I heard, my little sister, but the meaning is the same. When Mink comes back he can tell it to you in the right words."

"Tell it any way you can. I'm listening."

"It happened at the ocean," she said again. "There were strange things that appeared on the water. Do you remember the stories about the floating townhouses?"

I nodded.

"That is what they were. There were great cloths hanging above them, just as in the stories, and they suddenly appeared on the water and came closer and closer and then stopped a good distance out from the shore. The Chicoras came to the shore to look, and they could see things like humans walking around on the townhouses. They thought, 'Well, these are Immortals,' and they talked among themselves and decided to leave them alone because they were uncertain about their nature. But the Immortals lowered a dugout into the water and several of their warriors got into it and paddled toward the shore. This frightened the people, and they ran back and hid themselves, but still they watched, and the closer the Immortals came, the more the people were surprised at their strange appearance. The strangers wore peculiar clothing of bright colors, and some wore a kind of metal, like copper. They had let their hair grow long on their faces, and they were light, their skin was light, as if they had never been in the sun.

"The Immortals brought their dugout to the shore and got out and began walking around, looking toward where the people had run, and the people began to realize that the Immortals were at least a little frightened, because they would not walk far from their dugout. They would go just so far, and then turn and walk the other way, always staying close to the dugout. So the people said among themselves, 'These strangers look harmless enough. Perhaps someone should go speak to them.'

"Of course there are always a few warriors who will undertake anything, and two of them offered themselves and went out to greet the Immortals. Everyone could see what was being said because the Immortals used gestures that were large and awkward, and the warriors used them also because the common gestures seemed not to be understood. What happened was this: the Immortals invited the two warriors to come to their townhouse to meet their headman. The warriors talked it over between themselves and then agreed to go; and while the Immortals smiled toward the hiding people and nodded and waved, they got into the dugout with the two warriors and paddled back to their townhouse.

"The people watched them go, and no one knew what to think. The kinsmen of the two warriors were upset, but the beloved men urged everyone to be calm because the warriors had gone voluntarily. So the people waited and after a while they saw the dugout leave the townhouse and start back toward the shore. This time the Immortals did not come onto the shore. The two warriors got out and waded in, and the Immortals returned to their floating townhouse. But it was not a townhouse, the two warriors told the people. It was something that was entirely strange. They had asked the headman of the Immortals about it, and he had told them with gestures that it was a great dugout. The Chicoras laughed at this, and the warriors went on to tell them that the Immortals had invited all the warriors and beloved men to come out on the water to a feast.

"They talked that over with all the people. One of the two warriors suggested that they were dealing with strange human beings instead of Immortals. That idea was debated, but most agreed that it was impossible for the strangers to be humans, that there was nothing human about them except their form. Then someone pointed out that because the strangers were Immortals, the people could not go to their feast, because if a man eats spirit food it changes his nature and he cannot live anymore in This World. But there were many now who wanted to go. They had seen the two warriors go out and return without harm. So someone suggested that they take along their own food to eat. That was approved as a good idea. And so after a few days, more than a hundred men, almost all the warriors and beloved men who lived near there, got into their dugouts and went out to visit the great dugouts of the Immortals. The women sat on the shore and watched and waited. They saw their men climb into the great dugouts, and then they saw the huge cloths raised, and as they watched, the great dugouts began to get smaller, moving away, and they could see the empty dugouts of their men left floating free upon the water. The women were seized with fear and cried and wailed, but the great dugouts grew smaller and smaller in the distance and at last they disappeared."

Hawk Sister began to weep. I moved closer to her and put my arms around her. "Imagine their grief, my little sister," she sobbed. "They waited on the shore for days hoping their men would return, but they never did, and they still have not, though it has been longer than a month since it happened. Those poor women. To think that such a thing could ever happen. Such a terrible, terrible thing. What could it have been? Who were those strangers? Who *were* they?"

I felt a horror in the deepest part of me, a blackness in the center of my soul. "And what did they do to the men?" I whispered.

The people of the Seven Clans met in council that night and listened with distress to the story told to them by the two men from the Lower River. When the visitors had finished, Gray Hawk, the headman, rose to address the Seven Clans.

"You are my kinsmen," he began. "You are my mothers and my uncles, my sisters, my older brothers and my younger brothers, my nieces and my nephews, my grandchildren. We are all one people, one family, not only with ourselves and with the Seven Clans in other towns, but also with the Lower River People. They are our older brothers, just as they are the older brothers of the Chicoras. We are all within one circle, and on hearing such a story about the Chicoras, it is as if it happened to us, and the tears flow freely from our eyes. People of the Seven Clans, we are not here to decide a course of action, for there is none that is open to us. We cannot join our older brothers on a trail of revenge, for there is no trail that leads across the ocean. The Lower River People are powerless to act against such mysteries, and we are powerless to help them. Their priests are working to seek the meaning of the event and ours will do the same. Already our beloved men have pondered it, and as we all speak together here tonight, we will endeavor to draw ourselves into a unity of understanding. Let us begin to speak."

Gray Hawk took his seat. Mink rose as the first speaker in the circle. "Brothers and sisters of the Seven Clans! Older brothers of the Lower River People! I speak before you as your kinsman. Today I have listened to a tale of great sadness, and my heart has been full of dread as I have struggled to come to an understanding of it. Let us sit together and examine this mystery. Let us seek to find the center. Let us seek to understand the nature of the strangers, those who some say are Immortals. We have heard of them before. For several years we have heard stories of them, stories that until now have come from far to the south. In each story it is said that these strangers eat the same food that humans eat, that they come to shore and ask for human food. This is something that I have always found disturbing. Immortals do not have the nature of human beings—they would be destroyed by human food just as humans are destroyed by spirit food.

"And here is another thing. Immortals do not have it in their nature to appear befor throngs of people, but only before a solitary man walking through the mountains and the forests. And yet in all the stories we have heard of these ocean strangers, they have revealed themselves to whole towns of people.

"And now we hear also that these strangers come to the shore with fear in their hearts, that they are so frightened that they will not venture far from their dugouts. What is it that Immortals have to fear from humans? Humans cannot hurt them or gain any power over them. Brothers and sisters of the Seven Clans, I cannot believe that these frightened strangers are Immortals. But then who or what could they be? One of the warriors who went to their great dugouts and returned believed them to be human beings, and yet that also is difficult to believe. There seems to be little about them that is human except for their appetites and their fears. Brothers and sisters, I have no answer to these questions. I myself do not understand the nature of the strangers."

Mink sat down, and after a moment Bender rose to speak. "My beloved kinsmen! I wish to speak to you about Immortals. I wish to speak to you about their nature. I wish to remind you that though we do not know so much about the food of Immortals, yet we know a little more about the food eaten by the spirits of the dead. We know that we give them human food for their journey to the Darkening Land, and that they eat the essence of it. We know that if through negligence we leave food outside through the night, we throw it away in the morning and do not eat it because the ghosts of those wandering on this side of the Darkening Land might have eaten of it, and the nature of such food is changed and becomes dangerous to humans. And so to me it seems likely that Immortals could also make use of human food. This is no problem in my understanding. Brothers and sisters of the Seven Clans, the strangers as they were described to us could not have been human beings, and if they were not humans, then I think they must have been Immortals, perhaps of a different kind than we have here in the mountains."

The discussion continued and in time passed around the circle and came again to Mink. He spoke once more against the idea that the strangers were Immortals. But as the talk passed another time around the circle, going from one to another of the men and women who wanted to speak, the consensus seemed to be going against Mink. As it came to him a third time, he declined to speak, and those who supported him also declined, and this time the council reached consensus: the strangers were Immortals who had taken their captives away to live in the Lower World.

We went home afterwards, the three of us, very tired. I was saddened to see Mink lie down on a separate bed, apart from either of us. I went and knelt for a moment beside him, stroking his hair to soothe him. "Perhaps tomorrow we can walk together," I said softly.

"No," he said. "I think we should not." But then he wavered. "Perhaps a short walk, little wren."

We went early the next morning, the two of us together, walking through the green cornfields in the valley. I knew that things were not right between us, but when we spoke, it was as if they were.

"They did not see the truth last night," I said.

"No," said Mink. "I could not lead them to it. And what is the truth? I only tried to show them what it was not. Those strangers are not Immortals. But then, what are they? They couldn't be humans, could they? And it is reasonable to think that if they aren't humans, then they must be some kind of Immortals. I have to wonder if perhaps the others are not right."

"Is that why you let them carry the council?"

Mink did not answer. There was silence between us, a long silence as we walked through the summer morning. Then he said, "*Could* they be humans, little wren?"

My heart began to pound, some fear uncovered. "I believe you think they are. I believe that from the very first you've been disturbed by the stories because you are afraid that these are humans coming to the shores around us. I myself do not know, my husband, but I am frightened. If they are men, they are of a different kind. Their nature seems black and foul."

"They are the center of a black circle," Mink said quietly.

I stopped. "You mean the omens?"

"Yes."

"Then they have been fulfilled?"

"No," he said. "Not yet."

I breathed deeply, and then again, trying to calm myself.

Mink felt that we should return to the town, and we turned and walked back again through the summer morning.

SIX

Mink was afraid of losing his power—or if not his power, his influence. It was a defeat for him when the council went against him, when they listened to Bender—Bender, the dim-sighted seer of shallow truth. Mink knew the reason for it; he knew what they were saying about the two of us; and that was why he turned his back on me. Before the eyes of the people he shook himself free. He took his walks alone as he had before our marriage. He came for his meals, but he no longer brought the beloved men to sit at our fire. Often he would not come home at night but would sleep in the town-house to show the men how much he was free of my influ-ence. I would lie awake without him in the darkness, strug-gling to understand. I tried to tell myself that in his heart he did not mean it, that it was a show for the others. But I was not strong enough. I felt hurt and mistreated, and miserably alone.

It was then that I first began to notice Trotting Wolf, Mink's nephew. I was lonely, and when I would look up to see him coming into our yard, it would please me and I would say, "Your uncle is not here at the moment, but please come sit with the two of us." Hawk Sister would spread a mat for him in the place of honor, and we three would sit together and talk. Trotting Wolf's manner was so very solemn. I began trying to break through it, to make him smile. And I saw he had his uncle's smile, that elusive mirth that came from around the eyes. Perhaps at first it was the smile that drew me to him.

But there was also his gentleness. It mixed so oddly with his warrior qualities. Though the oldest of Mink's nephews, Trotting Wolf had not taken to priestly matters. He was instead a dedicated warrior, climbing relentlessly from one rank to another, never marrying, intent always on winning a higher name of honor. But he had never led a war party. "Not until my power is great enough," he told us. "The best war leaders never lose a warrior to the enemy. They are the ones whose stories live, whose songs are sung long after they are dead. It is no victory to parade home with a pole hanging full of scalps if even one of your party is missing. It is no victory if there are tears. The war leader who sacrifices the blood of a brother for a dance of glory does not deserve the praise of his people. He should come home hanging his head in shame." Trotting Wolf was that way, taking everything so very seriously.

I had known him all my life, a friend of my brothers, someone who was always there. Yet I had never noticed him, never listened to him, never looked at him long enough to see what he was like. Now I found my eyes wandering to this warrior, reaching into him. Perhaps he meant for it to happen. Perhaps he went to a priest and bought a song to draw my eyes into his soul. Certainly I was looking forward to his visits now, and he began to come more often and stay longer.

Then suddenly I was frightened. I could feel what was happening, and for the sake of Mink I did not want it. But when I tried to shut Trotting Wolf from my thoughts, it was like pushing back a waterfall. I knew then that he was singing songs to hold me. But I was strong and would not be held.

When he came the next time to visit, I greeted him differently. "Strange that you come so often expecting to find your uncle," I said to him. "Everyone knows that he is seldom home. I am sure you don't mind that I was just leaving to visit my mother." And with that I gathered up my work and left him there with Hawk Sister.

But at my mother's I felt worse than I could have ever imagined, so distracted that I could not work nor conduct the most simple conversation. I could think only of Trotting Wolf. I feared that I had done what I had meant to do, that I had put him off and he would not come to see us anymore.

"I suppose everything is all right with you," my mother said. She could not help but notice.

"I'm sorry, my mother," I heard myself saying. "We were to have a guest today—I forgot all about it. I have to return home. But I'll come again this evening so we can visit." And suddenly I had gathered up my things and was hurrying away, hurrying home, almost running to get there before he left. But when I arrived, Hawk Sister was alone.

"My mother and my grandmother were gone," I lied. "I talked to my father a little while and then came back. I guess Trotting Wolf couldn't stay long."

"Not long at all," Hawk Sister said. Then a silence. Perhaps she knew. I tried to think of something to say, something to obscure things. But that might only make it worse, so I spread a mat and sat down without saying anything. Hawk Sister hardly looked up. We both concentrated on our work.

The next day I was resolved again to be strong. Mink had slept at home that night—with Hawk Sister, not with me, but he had been lighthearted, joking with us, almost like it used to be. Perhaps things would be changing soon. So when Hawk Sister went that afternoon to visit her older sister, I moved inside the house so that if Trotting Wolf came by, he might think that I too was away.

But he knew. I did not hear him approach. When he ducked inside the door, I jumped to my feet in surprise. Seeing him, there was no more strength in me.

"Mink isn't here," I said weakly. "Nor Hawk Sister. The two of us should go outside."

He stood before the doorway, unmoving, looking at me with eyes I could not meet. Then he was walking toward me, silently, for an awful space of time walking toward me without a sound. I could not think but stood waiting until he was there, until he reached out and put his hands against my face. Trembling, I did not pull away, and an understanding passed between us. Then he turned and I followed him outside.

We sat at the fire, he on one side, I on the other. I offered him tobacco, Mink's tobacco, and he smoked a pipe of it before he spoke. "I am to lead a war party," he said at last. I looked up at him, startled. "I have consulted with the war priest," he said. "The signs are good, more favorable than they have ever been. It is time for me to lead."

Was this supposed to be good news? I felt only a chill. "Will it be against the Coosas? I've heard nothing of it."

"Last night they killed a child at Bear Hill. A child of my clan. I offered to lead a party, and eight men have agreed to follow. Tomorrow we go into seclusion with the war priest to prepare ourselves."

There was nothing I could say. I did not want him to go to war. Looking down, I toyed with the fringe on my belt.

"I will be responsible for eight men," he said. "If I lose even one, I'll not lead again."

"Do not lose yourself," I said softly, hurting in my throat.

For a long time there was silence. Then he said, "I want you to meet me tonight. It is my last night to be with a woman."

My heart raced. "I would be afraid," I whispered. "I could not bear for Mink to know."

"We will be careful. It is you I want to be with tonight."

"Where would we meet?"

"At the river. By the swimming hole."

"The swimming hole." I was trying to think, to be rational. "How could I get there? The guards would see me."

"Don't go straight to it across the valley," he said. "Go as if for water and then follow the river beneath the trees."

"You don't think Coosas will be waiting there for just such a thing?"

"No, I don't think there will be danger. But go very quietly, and listen."

"I will be there," I said, gathering myself together. "Just after dark I will be there."

Then he left. I was alone, waiting for the evening, terrified at what I was planning to do. What would I tell Hawk Sister? More lies? And if Mink came home to sleep instead of staying at the townhouse? I tried not to think about Mink, about how he would feel if he knew. What if he found us? I could not think about that. I could not. But perhaps if he found us, he would be pleased. Yes, pleased to have his problem with me solved. Lies! He would be pained, his own nephew stealing his wife. Still . . . he had thrust me aside, and I was too young to be thrust aside. Much too young. Even though in his heart he still loved me. But that did not matter now. Only Trotting Wolf mattered tonight. Trotting Wolf the warrior. He had found his way into the center of my soul.

The afternoon passed and Hawk Sister did not return. The sunset was red and beautiful. Now in the dusk it was obvious that Mink would stay at the townhouse. And so at last I took up a water jar and started for the river, leaving behind a lonely house, an empty yard. It was easier that way—if they did not care enough about me to come home.

Near the river I met two women returning with jars full of water. "We will wait for you, my younger sister," said one of them. "It is late to be going alone for water."

"You are kind," I replied. "But I will be bathing. I would not have my older sisters wait so long for me. There is no danger tonight. The Coosas have surely gone home after killing the child at Bear Hill last night."

Bathing after dark? They must have thought it strange. But one of them said, "What a pity to kill a child," and they continued on their way, leaving me to convince myself that the Coosas had indeed left our country. I could have believed it more easily had I been safe inside the palisade instead of alone out here, walking the paths in the dark.

When I entered the trees, the night sky was shut away behind the leaves and it was truly dark. Yet it was not a black darkness. I could see the path. And I could see into the trees where here and there the starlight filtered through, silhouetting the dark forms of the forest. I watched the shadows, looking for movement, listening for any sound that did not belong.

Leaving my water jar hidden in some brush, I started down along the trail to the swimming hole. Each step took me farther from the town, farther from the safety of the palisade and guards. And now Mink might be coming home. He would wonder where I was. He would ask Hawk Sister and she would not know. Then would he look for me? Would he go to my mother and then to my sisters and my friends? Would he find out from those two I had met on the path that I had gone late to the river? Would he come here and find me with Trotting Wolf? Or would he find me dead and bloody on the path, scalped by the Coosas? He would grieve terribly. Maybe Trotting Wolf would find me first. Would he weep to find me dead? Surely he would not let Mink see his tears. Surely he would spare him that.

My heart was beating so I could barely hear the night. But I whirled at a noise, a crunching sound behind me. Straining, I searched the darkness. Nothing moved. Probably an animal —a night creature hunting for food. But for a long time I stood listening, watching the blackness of the shadows.

There were only the night sounds now, nothing more sinister than a bullfrog's song. But I was longing for Trotting Wolf, for the safety of his arms. I turned and hurried on, walking faster, going quickly, too quickly perhaps to have listened, wondering if I had gone too far, if I had passed the swimming hole. In the dark the way seemed different. I fought against the terror rising in me and hurried on, knowing in some sane part of me that I had not passed the place, that I would soon be there.

Then suddenly he was standing in the path ahead, Trotting Wolf the warrior, waiting for me in the darkness. He came to meet me, reaching out his arms, and we clung together, alone and hidden in the night. All sense of danger flowed away. We were floating on a white wind, beyond all reach, on the south wind of peace and joy. I forgot the terror of my journey, forgot the sound that I had heard, the sound I was no longer listening for.

But Trotting Wolf heard it. He caught his breath and dropped his arms, reaching for the war club in his belt. I heard a footstep brush the ground behind me and spun around to see a dark form step toward us.

"It is as I thought," said a voice. I began to weep. It was Hawk Sister.

"Go on," she said to Trotting Wolf, speaking to him with authority, the wife of his uncle. "Leave us here alone."

Trotting Wolf looked at me to see what I would have him do. I looked away and nodded for him to go.

"Wait for me on the path," Hawk Sister said after him.

I had never felt such misery. I sat down and cried, unable to look at her. But she knelt beside me and put her arms around me to comfort me. "I saw you leaving with the water jar," she said. "I knew we had plenty of water."

"I don't want to hurt Mink," I sobbed. "Not him, not you, not anyone."

"But one does not change husbands without causing a little pain."

"No!" I cried, shaking my head. "I am not changing husbands!"

"Is that not what you are doing? Stop crying, my little sister, so we can talk. If you are not changing husbands, what are you doing? Is this just for tonight? Will you forget about him after this?"

"I don't know what I'm doing. I don't want to betray Mink. I don't want to do this to him. I know he cares for me. I know he has to do what he is doing. But I am too young to be thrust aside. I have no children. I have nothing."

"You have Trotting Wolf," said Hawk Sister.

She said it once, but I heard it echo a thousand times. "Yes," I said quietly. "It seems that I have. . . . Perhaps you are right. Perhaps I am changing husbands." Then I looked at her in sorrow. "What about you, my older sister? I can't leave you alone."

"I won't be so alone. I will have my husband home again."

I sat silent, without thought, miserable—and yet relieved. At last I said, "Then there only remains to tell Mink."

"Only that," said Hawk Sister. "He will not want to hear

it." She embraced me sadly and rose to her feet. "Wait here," she said. "I will send your young man back to you. If Mink comes home tonight, I will tell him you are at your mother's."

It was a hard time for me as I waited for Trotting Wolf's war party to return, hard, like the north wind blowing, like the wind of blue misery. Every moment, day and night, I was afraid for him, yet I could not let it show. Had I been his wife, I could have stood by the war pole and sung battle songs for him. But I was Mink's wife.

And what would I do when Trotting Wolf returned? Perhaps just take up my things and walk away. But that would be a hateful thing. I had to find some way to tell Mink. I wanted him to know that even in leaving I had tender thoughts for him. Even with the barrier he had put between us, even with Trotting Wolf now in the deepness of my soul, even with all of this, I still cared for Mink, and I did not know how to tell him what I had done.

Then one day Mink came home early from the townhouse. It was midafternoon, too soon for his evening meal, too soon for him to be coming home. I set the pot of tea on the coals. He sat beside the fire and watched it until it began to steam. Dipping out a gourdful, he sipped it slowly. I concentrated on the moccasins I was making. Hawk Sister did not lift her eyes from her weaving. No one spoke until at last he said, "Come walk with me in the valley, little wren." I was distressed, afraid he might be turning back to me. But I rose and went with him, and we walked out through the valley and up the river to our little cove in the northern hills.

As we went along he said nothing, and I did not try to break the silence. In the cove he motioned for me to sit down on the log that was there. Then he went and stood beside the stream and looked into the water. He began walking slowly along the bank until he reached the far edge of the cove, then he turned and walked back again, always watching the water. It was as if he had forgotten my presence there.

He knelt by the water's edge and began taking things from his medicine pouch. He spread a piece of white deerskin on the ground and in the center of it he placed a clear quartz crystal, a lovely stone that sent colors dancing on the skin in the moving sunlight. He rose and for a time stood looking at it. Then he walked again along the stream, up and back, talking to himself, moving his lips. His face began to look peculiar, strained. It was twisted into something unfamiliar. I stared at him outright, knowing he was no longer aware of me.

Now he took tobacco from his pouch and waded into the stream. Holding it in his left hand, he moved the four fingers of his right hand over it in a continuous circle. I heard him singing, too softly for the words to reach my ears. Then he came out of the water, the tobacco remade, infused with power. He took a little of it and sprinkled it over the crystal. The rest he put in a pipe, a small stone pipe carved in the shape of a falcon. With his back to me he squatted and made a fire, a single flaming splinter with which to light his pipe. Now he waded back into the water and stood smoking the pipe, blowing smoke to each of the four pathways, to the east, the south, the west, the north. Turning again to the south, he blew smoke four times in that direction. Then he sang a song. Four times he sang it, and on the fourth time I heard the words: "White Falcon, fly high. Look there with your far-reaching eyes."

Mink's eyes were closed. Silent now, he raised his arms and for a long time he held them out before him, to the south.

Then they fell to his side, and he turned slowly and came out of the water.

I thought he was finished. But he took up the crystal and waded again into the shallow stream, and once more he faced the south. I could not see his face, but I knew he was looking at the crystal as he held it up in the dappled sunlight. He was chanting now, his voice building, growing louder and louder, the words slurred, or else too ancient for me to understand them. But I was caught in his song. My eyes were drawn to the crystal as he held it aloft, turning it in the sun, catching the light. The crystal flashed in time with the song, a silent drumbeat as his chanting filled the forest, as it caught me and held me with him, spinning on the four winds, in the center, the very center of the world.

Then suddenly there was silence. His hand closed around the crystal. He moved slowly, coming out of the water, wrapping the little stone in the white skin, tucking it into his pouch. But in his face he was himself again. He came over and stood looking down at me. He said, "Your warrior will return, little wren, and all his followers with him. I have seen that it is so. Let your heart be no longer blue, but white with joy."

I looked up aghast, not knowing what to say. But he reached out tenderly and touched my face. "Go home now," he said softly, "and wait for your new husband. Tell Hawk Sister I will not be home tonight."

Then Mink turned and left the cove. He walked up into the mountains and did not return for seven days.

SEVEN

Trotting Wolf did return, and my marriage with Mink was dissolved. Trotting Wolf and I were married without ceremony. We went to live in my mother's house until Trotting Wolf and his brothers could build a house for me.

The success of my husband's first war party did not go unnoticed. He had no difficulty finding followers after that, and no difficulty finding cause to go raiding again. The Coosas were harassing us that year, killing a man near one town, capturing a mother and child near another. It seemed there was always word of some outrage. And with so much crying blood to be avenged, Trotting Wolf stepped forward time and again. He could choose his men carefully now from the many who wished to follow. He consulted with the war priests, moving only when all the signs were in his favor, turning back at any ill omen. He took every precaution, exhorting his men to do likewise, unwilling to risk a single life, to seek any victory that was not complete. Perhaps he was hearing in his heart the song men might someday sing aloud. Perhaps he too could hear it on the wind. . . .

Trotting Wolf the Warrior,
Man of the Deer clan,
On the East Wind he travels,
Red Pathway of victory.
Above others he stands,
Armed with courage,
Shielded by Thunder,
The Red Man himself
Walking with him. . . .

Each day he was away on one of his raids I would sit beside the war pole at dawn and at dusk singing the songs that women sing for their men, songs of bravery and victory and safe return. And every fourth day I would sing all night without ceasing, until Red Man's dawn found my throat sore, my voice but a whisper. No other wife was singing so much for her husband, and as Trotting Wolf consistently returned victorious, people began to say there was power in my songs, that I was part of his success. I was alarmed to hear it, remembering how people's talk had driven Mink away from me. But Trotting Wolf was not Mink.

"Of course your songs have power," he whispered as we lay in our bed in my mother's house. "That is why you sing them. I would not have you stop. Sing them louder if you wish, but never stop. Do you want to ruin me?"

I shook my head, laughing softly as he drew me to him in the darkness.

In the autumn there was a house of my own, a small one squeezed into a spot near my mother's. By then I knew a child was coming. "In the spring," the old women said. And when they saw how large I was growing, they told me, "You are carrying twins. The younger will have power."

When it was time for the twins to jump down, I moved into the women's house of my clan and there gave birth to two baby boys. After what seemed a long time of seclusion, my clan mothers took me to the river and washed me and my two babies, and I went home to Trotting Wolf. My husband was pleased with his family. His sister named our sons for us. The firstborn she called Red Wind, saying he would be a warrior like his father. The younger one she named Traveler. "He will go everywhere," she said. "Just like his father."

"But not to the ocean," I said. "He will never go there."

"The ocean?" said Trotting Wolf. "What will keep him from the ocean?"

"My wishes will keep him away. Have you forgotten what happened there? It was but a year ago."

"You mean the Immortals? By the time Traveler is old enough to go to the ocean, that will be nothing more than a story we tell around the fire, a long ago tale of the hundred men carried out to sea—the Hundred Men, taken to the Lower World, never to be seen again."

"No," I said. "It is not over. Those people in the great dugouts will be coming back."

"People?" he said in surprise. "You think they were people?"

"I don't know, my husband. But whatever they were, they will be coming back. I know they will. Have you forgotten the omens? Has everyone forgotten them?"

"The ones so long ago? Who knows what they meant? We can't be always hiding in our houses for fear that on this day they will be fulfilled."

"I know," I sighed. "It is true. I do worry too much. I have always worried too much about things, ever since I was a child. I have always been waiting for something terrible to happen. It is foolishness."

Trotting Wolf looked at me. For a long time he studied me and did not speak. Then he said quietly, "You are a rare woman, my wife. You see and understand what others cannot. But I wish you could forget those deep things you seem to know, those things that frighten you."

I smiled at him, pushing away the blackness. "Usually I don't think about them," I said. "It is all right."

"Here now, we should talk of other things," said my husband's sister. "We have just named these twins. It should be a happy occasion."

"And it is," Trotting Wolf said cheerfully. "Look here at our little Traveler. Can you see in him the power of a younger twin?"

I looked at the baby, so tiny on his cradleboard. "No," I smiled. "I cannot see it. But surely it is there."

Whatever Traveler's power, Red Wind did not share it. Before a year had passed, my firstborn died.

"Children die," my mother said sadly. "You must learn to expect it."

But for me it was a bitter thing. I wailed and mourned until no tears were left. Then we buried Red Wind in the earthen floor of our house, beneath my bed, and we went to the river with a priest and washed ourselves free of him. After that, we spoke of him no more, though sometimes I would think of him and my heart would ache.

Traveler was in his third year when I learned there would be another child. It was midsummer, and Trotting Wolf had to give up the war trail, for a husband's manhood is not in balance when his wife is pregnant, and it is dangerous for him to go to war. He did not mind it as much as I had feared, and for me it was certainly a relief to be free of worrying for his safety. The child would come in late winter, my grandmother told me.

I asked her, "Will it be a boy or a girl?" No one can ever say for sure—it depends on so many things—but old women are best at it.

"It will be a girl," she replied lightly. "This one will be a girl to take my place."

I laughed and hugged her. "Your place is far from empty, my grandmother."

My daughter was born on a cold night near the end of winter. My mother was there in the women's house to help me, and so was Full Moon Woman, an old midwife. "A beautiful girl," said Full Moon Woman, handing me the baby. "So eager to jump down."

"Yes," said my mother. "An easy birth. I will go now to tell your grandmother. She was worried about this one."

There were only three clan sisters with me in the women's house. Moon Shadow was with a newborn baby. Yellow Bird and Carries Wood were in their time of blood. It was a lonely time in the town. Most of the men were away on a hunt, a long hunt that had carried them far from the town, and Trotting Wolf was with them. Many of the women had followed in the hunting camp to dry the meat and dress the skins. Most of the older people remained, as did the young children and the pregnant women. There were also a few warriors who had stayed behind to hunt for us. As I lay in the women's house, I wished that Trotting Wolf had been one of them so that he could know sooner about his baby daughter.

It was the next evening after my child was born that we heard wailing in the town. "Someone has died," Moon Shadow whispered anxiously.

Carries Wood went to the door and looked out.

"Someone will come soon and tell us," I said.

We waited in silence, apprehensive, none of us wanted to guess about such a thing. Then Quail Moccasin, my mother's sister, came into the women's house. Her eyes were red from crying. "It is Cougar Woman," she told us. "Your grandmother is dead."

I gathered my baby into my arms and wailed softly with my clan sisters. But it was a gentle sadness. Cougar Woman had lived a long life.

After a few days, Yellow Bird's time of blood was over, and she left the women's house. But she returned the same day to visit us. "All of the news is not reaching this house," she said. "There is talk in the town."

"Have they heard from the men?" I asked.

"No, it is not that. It seems that there have been some travelers through the town. A man and a woman of the Seven Clans. They were down among the Lower River People, and they heard some things. It seems the great dugouts with the hanging cloths returned."

"The strangers! We must send for the men! Has someone gone to tell them?"

"No," said Yellow Bird. "Because the Immortals have already gone again. They took captives, but not so many as before. They stopped at every river and came onto shore and took one or two people. But that was all, and now they are gone. It was not so bad as before."

"I wish someone would send for the men," I said. "I wish Trotting Wolf were home."

"Mink says the hunt is almost over. Everyone will be home before the new of the moon."

"Mink is back? And Hawk Sister too?"

"Yes. Both of them."

"Is she well?"

"She seems so now. But they say she was ill in the hunting camp. That's why they came home early."

"Perhaps you will do something for me," I said. "Perhaps you will ask her to come tonight to see me."

"I will go now and tell her that you are asking for her," said Yellow Bird.

"Thank you, my younger sister. And thank you for bringing us the news."

I was asleep when Hawk Sister came. It was late, and the fire in the hearth was low. She added wood, and the crackle of it was enough to wake me, for I had been waiting for her even in my sleep. I opened my eyes and saw her there by the fire. "My older sister," I murmured fondly. "You are here."

She came and sat beside me on the bed, lifting the blanket to let the firelight fall upon the baby. "It is a beautiful child," she whispered. "Her father will be proud."

"We call her Little Cougar."

"Yes. I have heard."

"Have you heard also about the return of the strangers?"

"Yes," she said soberly. "I have heard that too."

"What does Mink say about it? I would like to know what he is saying."

"He says the strangers have a nature that is black and foul and that they should not be allowed upon our shores."

"Does he say they will return after this?"

"He says nothing else about it. Only that they are black and foul."

"How does he seem? Is he greatly disturbed?"

"He is disturbed. He walks alone and scarcely talks to anyone."

"I wish I could talk with him."

"Yes, my little sister. That would be a good thing."

"And I wish Trotting Wolf were home."

Hawk Sister smiled. "We saw him in the hunting camp. He was anxious for the hunt to be over. He was concerned about you. He missed his son and was wondering about the new baby."

I gave a sigh. "I wish the strangers had not returned, my older sister. It frightens me. I think they will keep coming back. And if they do, I do not know what will happen to us."

"Don't be thinking such things," said Hawk Sister. "You should rest now so that you will be strong when Trotting Wolf returns. You should be happy to have such a beautiful daughter."

"But I am afraid for her, too."

"Shh, my little sister. Don't talk like that. Things will seem better in the morning. Here now, I will sit with you until you sleep."

There came a summer, in Little Cougar's third year, when we were not at war with the Coosas, but neither were we at peace with them. We had not met with them to throw away our war clubs, yet there was a balance between us that summer, no crying blood. Some said the Coosas were busy fighting the people on the other side of them, to the southwest. Whatever the reason, we were thankful for it. In every townhouse of the Seven Clans the old men were exhorting the young warriors to keep the balance. Let not our warriors be the ones who undo it, the old ones entreated. Let our people have a rest. Let them fish up and down the river without fear. Let them swim in the deep places without always looking over their shoulders, without starting in terror at every sound. Let them walk the trails in safety—the hunting trails, the berry trails, the visiting trails to other towns. If the warriors should seek glory, let them find it in the ball game, the little brother of war. There will be other years for war honors. Let this one be a year of safety and rest.

So Trotting Wolf, unwilling to go against the beloved men, went north into the mountains that summer with Red Dog and some others of his friends to gather crystals and mica and fine flint. Then they turned south and a little east, a trading party now, and journeyed to the country of the Lower River People, to Big Town, where the river comes out of the hills to meet the low country. The traders told us not to look for their return until the second full moon after their departure—trading between friendly towns proceeds slowly; there are debts of hospitality to be repaid, and many more to be incurred.

But I was not lonely in my husband's absence. I had my brothers to hunt for me and keep me company. And with Trotting Wolf away, they spent more time than ever with my children—especially with Traveler, in his fifth year now, old enough for his uncles' attention. For Traveler it was an eventful summer. Two Crows took him on a journey, the two of them alone, up into the high mountains to see a nest of golden eagles. It was a secret nest that Two Crows had discovered, that no other man had seen. He was giving the knowledge of it to his nephew. They journeyed slowly, for Traveler was such a small boy and so much was new to him. They pushed up into the lonely places and came at last to the nest, near the top of a high mountain. Within sight of it they hid themselves and watched the eagles come and go, saw their beauty as they soared on the wind, felt their power. Then the two, my brother and my son, crept silently away, leaving the great birds undisturbed.

Little Buck was at my house the day they returned. His wife was there with him, and his baby son. And when Two Crows' wife, Rising Moon, heard that her husband was back, she came hurrying to join us, bringing along her two small daughters. My mother came too and my father, and also my mother's sister, Quail Moccasin. But it was not only to greet the returned travelers that they came: they all wanted to be there to see Traveler's face when Little Buck presented him the new bow.

"You can throw away your baby bow," Little Buck said to him after we had all eaten and the story of the journey had been told. "I have made you one like the big boys carry."

Traveler took the bow eagerly from his uncle—so small it seemed to us, and yet so large to him. Then Little Buck gave him the quiver of arrows that went with it. Two Crows helped him sling the quiver across his back, and Traveler took out an arrow and nocked it in the string.

"No more hunting beetles with a bow like that," said Little Buck. "What kind of game will you be shooting now?"

"Bears!" cried Traveler, yanking back the bowstring and letting fly a shot at the post next to Little Buck. We cried out, laughing, as Little Buck threw himself to the ground and the arrow passed barely over his head and landed harmlessly in the dirt beyond.

Two Crows reprimanded Traveler. "Your uncle is not a bear," he said—which set us laughing all the harder. "Nor is that post a bear. Perhaps you are not old enough for such a bow."

"I am old enough," my little son said quietly, hanging his head in shame. Then as proof he added, in a whisper, "I have climbed the mountains and seen the golden eagles in their home."

On a morning soon after, at the river with my clan sisters, I looked up to see a younger sister running toward us down the path. "They are coming home!" she cried. "The trading party sent a runner to say they are coming today!"

I came out of the water and dressed happily. Going upstream a little way, I filled my water jar and then hurried home. In the afternoon my brothers came to my house with their wives and children, and my mother and my father came, and Trotting Wolf's sister. They all wanted to see what Trotting Wolf would bring and hear the stories he would have to tell. We sat in the shade and waited. At last we heard a shout from the watchman on the palisade. Before long we could hear the noise as the trading party entered the town, and by the sounds we could trace the movement through the streets as the different travelers reached their homes. And then Trotting Wolf was coming to us across the yard, a heavy bundle straining against his shoulder.

"You have returned," I said, beaming with the pleasure of seeing him.

"Yes," he said. "It was a good journey." He put his bundle on the ground in the midst of us and sat beside it. "There is something here for everyone," he said as he opened the bundle. The children were crowding in, and he brought out boxes for them, little wooden boxes with pictures of animals painted on the sides.

"What shall we keep in them?" asked Two Crows' older daughter.

"Whatever is precious to you," said Trotting Wolf.

"Mine is a medicine box," said Traveler.

I looked at my little son in surprise. But my mother nodded knowingly. "The younger twin," she said.

"And this is for Rain Dove," said Trotting Wolf.

I gasped with pleasure as he handed me a length of mulberry cloth, beautiful white cloth with a pattern of red worked into it. "It is lovely," I said, holding it to my face to feel the beauty of it. "You will see me wearing it at the New Corn Festival."

"And what would this be?" said Two Crows, and he picked a strange object from the bundle. It was a wedge-shaped thing, something like an axe head. It looked to be made of copper, but it was not copper. It was a gray metal, dark.

"It came from the strangers," said Trotting Wolf. His eyes turned to me as he spoke. "They have returned. They are building a town at the mouth of the Lower River."

"A town!" exclaimed Little Buck. "And no one is stopping them?"

"The Chicoras tried, but many of their warriors were lost in the battle. There are hundreds of the strangers. How can hundreds be stopped?"

"They are not Immortals, are they." My voice sounded strange to my ears, my head swimming.

"No," he replied. "They are not Immortals. They are human beings. They are people. Strange, light-skinned people. They are building a town out of poles and mud and thatch. They mean to stay this time."

"Have you seen them?" asked Cries Victory.

"No, my father-in-law. I did not care to go near them. But scouts were sent from Big Town to keep an eye on them. Every day one of them came back with a report."

"Who has taken this news to Gray Hawk?" asked my father.

"Red Dog went straight to him. No doubt there will be a council tonight and everyone will hear the story. But perhaps I should finish showing you what I have brought. Then we will sit together and I will tell what I know."

I sat back, strangely calm, waiting while my husband gave cloth to his sister and shell to my mother. He gave stone pipes to my brothers and shell to their wives and ear spools to my father. Then he showed us what he had brought for others, for his mothers and his father, his uncles and his younger brothers and his clan sisters. And then he was finished. Everyone sat back and looked at him as he spoke.

"They came first to the river of the Chicoras," he began. "To the same place they came five years ago. They came in seven boats, but coming into the mouth of the river, one of the boats sank. It sank slowly, and all the people had time to get out, but the scouts told us there must have certainly been things in the boat that were lost to the strangers. But the other boats came in without trouble and all the people were soon on shore. There were hundreds of them. Enough for a large town. There were men and women and even children. All had skin very light in color, as if they had never been in the sun. Except that there were a few who were as black as night. The black ones seemed to be captives of the light ones —they were treated as slaves.

"The first thing the strangers did when they came on shore was to stand together behind a man who seemed to be their leader. They all watched him as he faced the trees beyond the shore and held a piece of white cloth in front of his face and looked at it while he gave a talk. The scouts who were hiding nearby and saw this said that it was as if he were talking to them, but the language was like nothing they had ever heard. After his talk, some of this man's warriors planted a staff in the ground. It was made of two pieces of wood that were crossed, and the scouts were not sure what it was for. They thought perhaps it was a war pole.

"Then the strangers set up camp. Some of the men began making another boat, perhaps to take the place of the one that sank, though this new one was much smaller and was not covered over like the others. When they were finished, they put a pole in the middle and hung a cloth on it. In the meantime, some of the men had gotten back into two of the boats and had left. One of the boats went one way along the shore and the second one went the other way. And at the same time, a few of the men had set out in opposite directions along the inland trails, perhaps as scouts, although they did not move very quietly.

"Before very many days had gone by, the two boats returned, and soon afterward the scouts. Then all the women and children got back on the boats, and some of the men, those who had fallen ill, were taken on with them, and all the boats went away. The rest of the men set out on land and came down the coast toward the mouth of the Lower River. The boats with the women were there to meet them, and it became clear that this was the place they had chosen for their town. The last word we heard before leaving Big Town was that the strangers had begun to build houses."

"Did they bring food with them?" asked my mother. "What will they eat in the winter? It is too late to plant."

"They seem not to have much food. They sent messengers to some of the towns nearby to ask for some, but no one would talk to them. Everyone ran, remembering how before they had come to take captives. But then the strangers caught a woman, and instead of taking her captive, they treated her kindly. They dressed her in some of their clothing and sent her back to her people, telling her, as best she could understand it, that they wanted corn and that they would trade for it. But the people still did not trust the strangers and continued to avoid them. They remembered how the Chicoras had been tricked before. And the woman would not keep the clothing they gave her. She threw it in the river. The people killed the next messenger the strangers sent, and I think they sent no more after that."

"What of the men the strangers captured on their earlier raids?" asked Little Buck. "Did they bring any back with them?"

"We heard later that there were a few with them when they first landed. Only a few. The scouts from the Lower River People did not notice them because they were dressed like the strangers. We heard from the Chicoras that the captives had learned the language of the strangers and that the strangers wanted them to act as interpreters. But on the very first night they stripped off their strange clothing and escaped and returned to their homes."

"What is so strange about their clothing?" asked Day Moon. "What does it look like?"

"I am not very clear about it, my mother-in-law. It seems that the men wear leggings and heavy moccasins. And beneath their capes, they wear a cloth wrapped separately in some manner around their chests and arms. Like leggings, I suppose. And sometimes the men wear clothing that is made of metal. I have heard the scouts try to tell about it, but I do not understand what they are describing. The women, it seems, go around always with their breasts covered, and also every bit of their legs are covered with long skirts that reach all the way to their feet. And there are two or three men among them who go about dressed as women. Their skirts are always black, but the other people wear brighter colors."

"That is too much clothing," said Two Crows. "How could they move quickly in war? How was it that they defeated the Chicoras?"

"It is not a pleasant thing to tell," said Trotting Wolf. "You see, from the very first, the Chicoras had intended to fight them. The strangers owed them more than one hundred lives for the men they took away as captives in their boats. But the Chicoras were in no hurry. They wanted to watch the strangers and see what they were like and devise the best plan for attacking them without having more losses of their own. But then came that day the strangers broke camp. All the women and children got onto the boats and left, and then the men started out on land along the southern trail. The Chicoras didn't realize that they were moving no further than the Lower River. They knew only that they were leaving and that they had taken none of the lives which were owed to them. So they drew up a hasty plan for an attack on the trail. They didn't know that the strangers could use their beasts in battle."

"What beasts?" said Little Buck.

"They brought strange animals with them, like deer, the scouts said, only larger. And the strangers command them as if they were dogs. They fasten things onto their backs for seats and climb onto them and the animals carry them wherever they want to go. It is a very strange thing. The Chicoras had seen the beasts, but they did not know that they would carry their masters into battle. If not for the beasts, it would have been a good attack, for the strangers were caught completely by surprise. But all at once the ones on the beasts came charging into the Chicora warriors, bearing down on them with spears and long, slashing knives. Who could stand against such as that? The Chicoras were terrified. They tried to flee, but many were killed before they could escape. In the end, the Chicoras were lighter in the balance than ever. And now they have despaired of ever setting the matter straight."

We sat quietly together, each looking away in silence. I did not know what the others were thinking, but I myself was remembering the fourth omen, the Immortals riding before Mink on the backs of deer, laughing at him, mocking, and some of them, the ones who cared more about men, weeping and mourning. And now we were hearing that the strangers went into battle on the backs of beasts. Now we were being drawn at last into the dreadful circle of omens. It had finally come. I felt the sky pressing down on us, crushing us against the earth.

I turned anxiously and looked for my children. In the distance, it seemed, my father was speaking, saying, "It is not right to let so great a matter of blood go unsettled." My son and my daughter were inside the doorway of our house playing with their wooden boxes. Little Cougar reached her hands into hers and strained, lifting something from it, lifting it so I could see, holding up the strange metal wedge in her baby hands.

I jumped up and ran to her. I heard myself screaming. "No! No-o-o!" I was flying to her, grabbing the metal thing from her and flinging it away, feeling only the coldness of it, the dark, black coldness. Then I was lifting my child into my arms and holding her tight against me, and in her, too, I seemed to feel a coldness. I stroked her hair, knowing from her sobs that I had frightened her.

There was a slow circle of time in which nothing moved. Then my husband got up and walked across the yard and leaned over to pick up the metal wedge.

"Please do not," I whispered, pleading.

Raising up, he turned and looked at me. "It is only a piece of metal," he said softly. "It is nothing."

"It is black and foul," I said to him. "I do not want it in my house. I do not want it near my family. It came from those strange people who hide from the sun. It is unclean and will bring us misfortune. I do not want it near us. I do not want to see it anymore."

Trotting Wolf shook his head. "It is just a piece of metal. That is all it is."

I did not reply. I caressed my daughter and put her back on the floor with her brother.

"I will let Red Dog have it," said Trotting Wolf.

I looked at the others in the yard and saw them talking quietly among themselves, looking at the things Trotting Wolf had brought, trying not to notice that I was behaving so peculiarly. Trotting Wolf saw me looking at them. He caught my eye, and we both smiled. I was glad to have him home.

"We should all eat something," I said. "Then we can go to the townhouse."

"A fine plan," Trotting Wolf said cheerfully. He tossed a piece of deerskin over the metal axe.

EIGHT

Before winter had passed, the light-skinned strangers were gone. They limped away in their boats, more than half of them dead in that short time from starvation and disease. Even their leader had died, and they put his body in the little open boat they had made and towed it behind them as they sailed out into the sea and disappeared forever. They had been too ignorant to know how to live in our land. But they were hateful in their leaving. We heard that they had poisoned the waters of the people living near the shore. We heard that the people there died in great numbers, that more people died than lived. It was too awful a thing, and I was not certain I believed it. Sometimes the stories we hear are twisted from being told and retold before they reach us.

Then came another summer and we forgot the strangers as tragedy fell upon us. Coosas shattered the peace of our town. No one knew how they had done it. Our warriors had searched the trees on both sides of the river before the boys went to the swimming hole that day. They had searched the trees, and guards had been stationed on the far side of the river, and the watchman on the palisade had a clear view of the approach from the town side. So no one knew how the

Coosas made their attack. It was a terrible thing. Five of the boys were killed and also the young warrior who had been there to look after them. Our guards heard their cries and came rushing to them, filling the air with war whoops, and the Coosas fled, leaving two of the boys terrified but unharmed.

For days the town swayed with the wailing of mourners. Never had we been struck such a blow. We were dazed by the ferociousness of it. Anger swirled around the fires, and a war party of revenge was organized, a party larger than any that had ever gone out. Trotting Wolf was to lead it. He was the leader who had never lost a warrior, and he was the one to settle this very great matter of blood. He was to go against the Coosas leading twenty-three men. My brother Little Buck was among them. Even more men had stepped forward, but for various reasons Trotting Wolf had asked them not to come: Two Crows was tainted too much with the womanhood of his pregnant wife. "And besides," Trotting Wolf had said, "your brother's wife and your sister will be here without men; someone needs to hunt for them."

So Two Crows was not to go. But then my father's sister died. Turkey Woman had been ill for several months, and she died on the day before the warriors went into seclusion to prepare for the war trail. Her father, Crazy Eyes, so old now that he could not leave his bed, called his son Cries Victory to him. "Two Crows must leave the town," he told my father. "And Little Buck must go also. Running By is grieving for his mother, and he will be wanting to settle that old matter of blood. He has never forgotten the killing at the ball ground, and he will try now to send a Bird spirit along with his mother on the trail to the Darkening Land. My two grandsons should leave the town until we have found some other way to settle it."

When Trotting Wolf heard this, he agreed that Two Crows must join his war party after all. But first the war priest took my brother to the river and sang special songs for him while Two Crows washed himself clean of the influence of his pregnant wife. He slept that night in the townhouse to be away from her, and the next day he went with the warriors into the isolation of the warriors' house.

When the day came for the war party to go out from the town, I joined the other women in singing songs to stir the men to courage, songs to send them into battle without fear. Then I went home to my children and tried not to worry. Over and again I reminded myself that Trotting Wolf had never lost a single warrior.

With so many men gone, it was a hard summer for the town. Because of the attack by the Coosas, the guard force had to be kept strong, and that took the most able of the men who were left—a few warriors, the oldest of the boys, and the youngest of the older men. The women had little help in the fields, and meat for the cooking pots was scarce. But we did not complain. It was right that so great a matter of blood was being settled with the Coosas. And we knew that the men would soon be returning.

After a month had gone by and they had not returned, we began to say, They must have struck deep in Coosa country to be taking so long. That is good. It is more humiliating for the Coosas if we strike deep.

Then two months were gone, and we began to wonder. We said to each other, The Coosas must have come on their heels after the attack. Our men must have had to circle to lose them. Surely they will be home in time for the New Corn Festival.

But we had the festival without them. And instead of being a happy time, it was a dreary affair because we were worried about the men. I began to see women with eyes red from crying. And during the pole ball game between the men and the women, with the men's team made up of so many boys and older men, one of the women broke down in sobs, and we stopped the game. No one had the heart to finish it after that.

Then the summer was gone, and the leaves turned gold and red against the clear blue sky. The corn and the pumpkins were gathered in, and it was chestnut time. And suddenly I realized that the war season was truly over. My heart filled with despair. I did not know how long to wait before I, too, took down my hair and began to mourn.

For a while yet, I held back my grief, telling myself that this terrible thing had not really happened. And yet I could not deny that I was facing the winter alone with two small children. I did not know what I would do. My father was afflicted with arthritis and could not hunt for me. My clan brothers who were left in the town shared with me what they brought in, but so many other clan sisters were also depending on them for meat. Sometimes Running By would bring meat to my father, and Cries Victory would offer it to me. But I would never take it. I would starve to death before I would take meat that Running By had killed.

Then one day I looked up from my work to see Mink coming into my yard. In the six years since I had left him, we had spoken very little, though it was not because of bitter feelings. Now I greeted him awkwardly, but with gladness, spreading a place for him by the fire. He sat down and I gave him some pumpkin and hominy stew. "There is a little meat in it," I said.

"It is good."

When he had finished, he set the bowl aside, and for a long time he sat looking into the fire. Then he said, "My nephew has not returned. It grieves me. And for you I grieve even more. Your husband is gone, and both your brothers, and here you are alone with your two children."

I managed a little smile. "Have you come to make me cry?"

"No, my little wren. I have come to ask you to come with your two children to Hawk Sister's house. I am still getting meat for my curing. Not as much as before the men left, but there is enough to share. Come live with us. Your father is unable to take care of you, and you should not be here alone."

"You are kind to think of me. But I cannot take another husband. I have a husband. Or if I do not, then I am a widow and I must mourn."

"I am not asking you to come as my wife. You are the wife of my oldest nephew. You are a clan sister of my wife, and your children are her clan children. And you are alone with no one to care for you. Is that not reason enough to ask you into our home? I do not ask to be your husband. I ask only to have you to talk to, as I did once before. Only that."

For a long time I sat in silence. At last I shook my head. "I do not know what to say. You must give me time to think about it."

The leaves were falling from the trees, coming down in showers with the wind when I moved back to Hawk Sister's house. She greeted me warmly, holding me tightly in her arms. Then she hugged Traveler and Little Cougar, squeezing them until they squirmed to get away. It was clear that we three were welcome. We were wanted here. They would shelter us, Mink and Hawk Sister. They would hold me up in my grief, support me as I turned now to face it, as I let loose my hair, ran my hands through it, pulled and twisted it in agony, as the earth upended and crashed back upon me and I saw in my mind what must be true: my dead husband, my dead brothers, scalped and dismembered, trophies on the war poles of our enemies. They were dead, no more to stand before me, to walk alive upon the earth. I could see it now. I had to see it. Trotting Wolf was lost to me, lost forever, my beloved husband, no more to feel him, see him smile, lie in his arms, love him in the night. This wailing was not enough, this grief, these tears. Nothing could be enough, could let out the pain, could stop the earth from crashing. But Mink was there, and Hawk Sister. They held me up, gave me shelter and support until the sight of screaming death began to fade, until the earth stood level beneath my feet and I could feel once more the cool wind of autumn on my face and the sun warm upon my shoulders.

And coming to myself again, I began to look around, to see things that I should have seen before. Hawk Sister, for all the comfort she was giving me, was not well. She had aged in the years since I had left her, aged far more than Mink. Almost every day she took to her bed, seldom relieved now from her illness. Some days she did not get up at all. I wondered how they had been getting along here alone. Mink must have been cooking and doing much of the work for her. When I asked him about it, he said, "I have been asking for cooked food in payment for my curing. Then we have only to heat it."

"You do not need to do that anymore," I told him. "I will do the cooking from now on."

It was a new life, yet in so many ways it was familiar. My children were happy. Mink and Hawk Sister paid them attention. There had never been children in that house before, and though Traveler and Little Cougar sometimes made things confusing, I think Mink and Hawk Sister enjoyed them and were glad to have them with us. I took over the running of the house, working harder than I ever had, for it eased the pain. It was not long before the beloved men were sitting once more at Mink's fire.

Then the day came when Mink asked me to go walking with him in the valley. I hesitated. "Would it be wise?" I asked him. "Will they say again that I am robbing you of power?"

"They won't say it again. They regard you differently now. They saw you with Trotting Wolf and they had to say that you were helping him."

"That was before he lost everything, even himself. What do they say about me now?"

Mink's face darkened. "Nothing," he said. "They say nothing. And I will not allow it if they try. This time I will stop them."

So we went out into the valley, the two of us together, walking across the brown fields to the tree-lined river. Taking the upstream trail, we kicked our way noisily through the deep leaves, newly fallen and crisp on the path, and our hearts began to lighten. "We sound like bears going along," chuckled Mink.

When we came to the stream that ran into the river, we turned and followed up along it until we came to the little cove. The old log was still there. I sat upon it, feeling how it had softened from years of rotting. Mink sat beside me and for a time we did not speak. I looked at the cove, at everything around it, at Mink sitting beside me. "It is as it used to be," I said. "So long ago."

"And yet nothing stays the same, does it?"

There was a long silence, deep and thoughtful. Then he said, "It was good the way it used to be. I know that it was good. There was no strife between us, never any struggle to win something from the other. It was a deep thing, and I was wrong to have spoiled it. I will not spoil it again."

I walked now with Mink every day in the valley, as once I had done before. We talked deeply, about ourselves, about the town, about the greater forces of the world. We tried to understand things. We tried to understand about Trotting Wolf, what could have happened that the entire war party had been lost. "Why didn't the Coosas let one come back to tell the fate of the others?" I asked.

"Perhaps they did," said Mink. "Perhaps he was killed by someone else on the way."

"If they had let Trotting Wolf go, he would have killed himself before coming home. He had never lost a man. He could not have faced us after losing all of them."

"He was a great war leader," said Mink. "It is hard for me to imagine what could have gone wrong for him."

"Have you been thinking about the omens?" I asked him.

"About the warriors' tree?"

"Yes. About that."

"I have thought about it. But the omens were a circle drawn around the strangers. I have always felt that. And now the strangers have gone."

"Then why did the omens come to us? Why did they not come to the people near the ocean? They are the ones who suffered from the strangers."

"We are all brothers in this part of the land, from these mountains to the ocean. The Lower River People are the older brothers of the Seven Clans. They give the strength and protection of older brothers. And they are the older brothers of the Chicoras, and so the Chicoras are also our brothers. When the omens came to us, it was the same as if they had come to them. That is the way with brothers."

"And yet look at us here. Look at us with all our warriors dead. We have never known anything like this. What could have happened to them? Can we look at this and truly say that the omens were not meant for us?"

Mink shook his head, not knowing.

It was early in the winter when we learned at last about the invisible fire. We learned about it from two of our hunters who had wounded an elk and had followed it for four days through the hill country, south toward the Lower River People. When the elk tired and dropped, the hunters came upon it and killed it. Then, being far from home, they made camp and began to smoke and dry the meat. A lone hunter from Big Town, on the Lower River, saw their camp, and recognizing them as younger brothers from the Seven Clans, stopped to spend an evening with them. Our hunters saw that the skin of their older brother was badly scarred, as if he had been burned in a fire, especially on his face, which made him rather ugly. But they were polite and did not speak of it. They did, however, ask about his people. No visitors from the Lower River had come among us since early summer, not even to invite us to their New Corn Festival. We had thought it was because they were mourning their brothers and sisters who died of the poisoning near the ocean.

"It was not poison," said the hunter. "It was this." And he pointed to his scars.

Our hunters did not understand.

"Poison does not travel upstream," said the hunter. "And yet the death has been moving upstream, spreading through one town and then another. You cannot imagine what it is like. You cannot imagine how much death there can be in one place. You cannot imagine the groans that fill the air, the suffering and the agony. It falls on everyone, and soon there is no one who can stand, no one who can give water to the dying. It is like a fire that sweeps through the town, an invisible fire. People begin to fall with fever, and blisters rise on their skin and turn to running sores, and there is no way to give them comfort. When they move in their beds, the skin pulls away, and in time they are caked black with blood, swollen and disfigured, until you cannot even recognize in them your own brothers and sisters. I do not know why I myself am not dead. All my family is dead except one sister. And my wife's brother is alive. The three of us are living alone about a day's journey from Big Town. No one is in Big Town any more. Everyone who lived through the fire has scattered. I do not know what will happen to us—we are still living as if in a nightmare. Sometimes when I am alone hunting in the woods, it all begins to seem as if it did not really happen. But I look at my arms and see the scars and I know that it was real. Then I feel like a crazy man because I cannot understand what has happened to me."

Our hunters were shocked and frightened by the man's story. And they were filled with sorrow for the Lower River People. They gave their older brother a large portion of the elk meat, and then they hurried home to bring the news.

It was evening when they arrived and the Seven Clans were meeting in council. The two hunters came into the townhouse and spoke briefly with Gray Hawk, telling him they brought terrible news from the Lower River People. Gray Hawk asked that they tell it to all the council, and we listened aghast as they related to us what the man from Big Town had told them.

I reeled at the force of it, horror-struck, unable to imagine it. I heard the hunters' words but saw only the omens, the four omens moving around us in a circle. I saw them clearly, each one of them, as clearly as Mink had ever seen them, circling around us in the townhouse: the hawk rising with the snake, the snake writhing and turning and striking into the heart of the hawk; the warriors' tree burning, an orange glow across the valley under soft, drizzling rain; Ancient Fire dead in the townhouse hearth, Shaker beating his head against the post; Immortals on the backs of deer, laughing, except some of them crying, some weeping and mourning.

I looked for Mink across the townhouse, searched for him through the flickering shadows of firelight. I found him looking back at me in sorrow.

After that Mink began to leave the town—gathering medicines, he told Hawk Sister—and he would be gone for days at a time. But he was not gathering medicines. He was seeking knowledge about the invisible fire, talking to people who had heard about it, sometimes finding a person who had lived through it, who had fled up the river in horror as if to leave the memory behind. When Mink returned from these trips, the two of us would walk together beneath the winter skies, and he would tell me what he had learned. I could listen. I found that no matter what he said, I could listen. Even when he told me that the fire was sweeping toward us up the river.

"Maybe it will pass us by," I said. "Maybe there is something we can do."

Mink shook his head. "It has not spared a single town, not a single homestead on the way. Those who have tried to flee have taken it with them, or if they have fled before it, it has found them. The more I learn of it, the more I stagger beneath the weight of it. I walk along the streets of our town, sorrowing, looking at these people I have always known. I think to myself, Will you soon be dead? And you? Beloved brother, will you soon be covered with running sores? And you, dearest child, will you die in a room of dead people with no one to give you water for your thirst?"

"Do not talk like this," I pleaded.

"These are my people, Rain Dove. Gray Hawk is the headman, but *I* am the one they look to. They will beg of me to turn back the fire, and then what will I do? Is my power strong enough to deal with such a thing? How can it be? No one yet has had such power. In many towns the people have turned on their priests; they have put them to death, blaming them for the fire, screaming out that their power has turned black and destructive. But killing the priests has not stopped the fire."

"Our people wouldn't turn against you," I said. But I held my arms tightly against my knotted stomach.

"I am trying to get ready," said Mink. "I am trying to do what I can for them. I am fasting. You can see I have been fasting. And I am continually purifying myself. With the knowledge I have been gathering, perhaps I will find a way to work against it. But I am not sure that I can. What is one man against the fire of the Sun?"

When he heard that the invisible fire had come into the country of the Seven Clans, Mink asked Gray Hawk to call a council. The people of Mulberry Town came into the townhouse and divided into clans, each moving to his proper seat, all the clans in order, forming a circle around the light of Ancient Fire. The pipes were brought out and set before Gray Hawk, and he smoked from them and passed them around the circle of the Seven Clans, the beloved men of each clan smoking from them to bring the people together into one mind. Then Gray Hawk rose to speak.

"Beloved kinsmen of the Seven Clans! I am your brother

and your uncle and your grandfather. By your consent, I am the headman of our town. By your consent, I am the Keeper of Ancient Fire, which is the breath of our town. But for a time I have been wondering if perhaps I have gone to sleep and awakened in a different town, in the Lower World, perhaps, where things are more difficult to understand. Can this be Mulberry Town with so many warriors gone, with so many husbands and brothers and nephews vanished from our midst? Can this be Mulberry Town with a fire sweeping toward us from the Lower River? An invisible fire that threatens to destroy us? It is like a dream. We have been walking about with a deadness in our souls, waiting to awaken to the town we have always known. But our beloved brother Mink has not been doing this. Our beloved brother has been fasting and purifying himself to strengthen his power for this strange time. He has been walking the trails to the south of us and listening to the stories of others. He has come to an understanding of the nature of the sweeping fire. It is from this knowledge that he will speak to us now."

Gray Hawk took his seat, and Mink rose and stepped forward into the circle of firelight. He was thin from fasting, and the moving light showed lines of weariness in his face. "Beloved people of the Seven Clans! Some of you are my mothers and my uncles. Some are my sisters and some my older brothers and my younger brothers. And some of you are my nieces and my nephews. I stand before you as your kinsman and ask you to walk with me along the path of truth. It is not an easy way. Our hearts will grow fearful as we go along. But we must not falter. We must go bravely, for there is no way for us to turn aside.

"Beloved people of the Seven Clans! There has never been another time when so little word has passed between our older brothers on the Lower River and ourselves. We know only that a great misfortune has befallen them. And knowing it, we do not speak of it except to shake our heads as if this sad affair belongs only to them and will not come to us. But they are our brothers. They are our older brothers beneath the Sun, and the fire that swept across their towns has now come into the country of the Seven Clans. It is coming toward us from the south. Perhaps it will pass us by. Perhaps it will sweep around us without touching us.

"But it has not yet passed by a single town. It has not spared one homestead in its path. Yet I am working to keep it from us. I am doing everything I know as a priest to invoke cool forces to help against the fire, to call Thunder against the Sun. I am sure that the other priests will be working also. And all of you must take extra care in everything you do. We must follow more closely than ever the Beloved Path laid down for us in the Ancient Days of our people. And do not ever forget that the priests are working for you. They are not your enemies. If they cannot keep the fire from us, it is not they who are to blame. It is you yourselves who have acted to spoil the Sun.

"You will now be asking me to explain this thing. Why should it be coming toward us? What have the Seven Clans done to spoil the Sun? What did the Lower River People do, and the Chicoras, who have also felt the fire? For this I have fasted and purified myself and wandered to lonely places seeking answers. I have come to understand it. I have come to know that it is a matter of crying blood. It has been almost seven years since the strangers first came and stole away the hundred men. Chicora men. The Chicoras are the younger brothers of the Lower River People. The Seven Clans are the younger brothers of the Lower River People. We are all brothers together beneath the Sun. Had it been the Coosas who had taken so many men from the Chicoras, we would have joined with the Lower River People to seek revenge. We would not have rested until we had set the matter straight. But against the strangers we did nothing. The Chicoras made one attack against them and failed. After that they did nothing. The Lower River People did nothing. The Seven Clans did nothing.

"We all told ourselves that the strangers were different, that with them a matter of blood could not be settled. Why did we say that? They were humans—did they not die on our shores? They died, but we did not kill them. They died of their own ignorance and weakness, and their deaths did nothing to avenge the crying blood of our brothers. The Sun is the grandparent of us all. To have let such a great matter of blood go unsettled has spoiled the Sun against us. We are as much to blame as the Lower River People, and I see little hope that we will not feel the fire.

"Therefore, my beloved kinsmen, we must speak now of what we shall do if the fire comes to us. I have learned that when someone is burning from it, something changes inside his heart. Something makes him spread the fire to those around him. It is not a willful thing. Even a baby will spread it to his mother. So here is something I have been thinking about: suppose we find one among us burning from the fire. Suppose we send him out of the town to stay alone in a hut we have built for that purpose. Suppose we let him have no visitors, but let him recover or die on his own. If it were you or I, we would think it a hard thing, but suppose it kept the fire from touching others in the town. It is something I have been thinking about. I would like to hear now from you who are my kinsmen."

Mink moved back from the light and took his seat. The next one to step forward was Bender.

"Beloved people of the Seven Clans! Our brother has stood before us and spoken words to terrify our hearts. If there is a fire sweeping into the country of the Seven Clans, why has no one come to tell us? Is there anyone among us who has seen this fire with his own eyes? Are we to go home and weep in our beds because of some unfounded rumor? I think we are shaken by the loss of our war party. I think that if the warriors had returned, we would not be here talking about such strange things. But let us suppose that our brother is right about this. Let us suppose that everything he says is true, that one day I will awaken to feel this invisible fire sweeping over me? What if I do not want to go out of the palisade and stay alone in a hut? What if I want to stay in the safety of my bed and have my brothers bring a priest to cure me? Who is there who can compel me to leave my own house? I would like to hear an answer to this question."

As Bender returned to his seat, Gray Hawk rose to his feet. I had never seen his face so terrible.

"My beloved people! There is no one who can compel you to follow the advice of our beloved brother Mink. No one can force you from your beds and from the town. But we have heard that the fire puts a blackness in the soul that causes the burning person to pass his affliction to his friends and kinsmen. Only a witch with a twisted heart would not want to be saved from such a hideous thing. Only a witch would want to stay in the town to afflict other people." He turned and looked at Bender as he spoke. "I hope there are no witches among us. We have never dealt kindly with witches.

"Our brother Mink has fasted and purified himself and worked hard for us in this thing. We can all look at him and see how hard he has worked, how much he has fasted. He has learned the nature of the invisible fire. He has given us a plan to use in fighting it. Let our talk move now around the circle. Let us all agree that when the fire comes to us, we will deal with it as he has said."

The next day a hut was built in the trees beside the river.

NINE

Red Dog was out hunting when he met a man running up the trail from Bear Hill. The man was of the Seven Clans, from Blue Valley, and he had gone that morning to Bear Hill to visit kinsmen. But he found the town in disarray, the people dying, burned by the unseen fire. He tried to look for his kinsmen, but then his courage left him and he fled in terror. After speaking to Red Dog, the man went on, running home to the safety of Blue Valley. Red Dog turned at once and came back to Mulberry Town. That was how we learned that the fire had come to Bear Hill. And that, I believe, was how the fire came to us. Red Dog, without knowing it, brought it into the town. But others do not agree, for neither the man from Blue Valley nor Red Dog had felt the fire on that day.

For almost half the circle of the moon we waited, knowing that it would soon come to us. The fire had not yet missed a town. We would be next after Bear Hill. Most of us had kinsmen in Bear Hill, but we did not speak of them. We did not speak at all about the fire. We waited. We wondered silently how it would be, which of us would first be burned and have to leave the town to die alone in the hut. We tried to think of how it would be afterward, after the fire had left, for everyone thinks until the moment of his death that he will live through everything, that he will live to be old.

Mink was fasting continuously now, always weak from hunger. And every day he plunged into the freezing waters of the river, purifying himself, building his power. In the evenings he met with the beloved men, but there was little mention of the fire. They talked about the meat hunger in the town. Warriors were hunters, and so many of our warriors were gone. In the summer the belly does not think so much of meat—it is not so terrible to do without it. But in winter when there is no meat in the stew, the children cry, and their mothers look hungrily at the dogs sleeping by the hearth. So the beloved men talked of the meat hunger. And we waited.

Wakened from sleep one morning by wailing, I rushed out into the frozen dawn. In the yard I found Hawk Sister, a bundle of firewood in her arms, her feet rooted in the spot where she was standing. She stared ahead, listening to the wailing, clutching the firewood against her.

"It has come," I whispered, and the firewood dropped and lay scattered at her feet.

There were three who awoke that morning with the burning fever of the fire: Red Dog and one of his brothers and his brother's wife. The three left the town quickly, not protesting. And we waited anxiously, hoping that no one else would be touched. I told my children to stay near home, and often I would feel their faces, finding comfort in the coolness that was there. But by evening, two others had the fever, Red Dog's wife and one of her sisters' children. The two left the town in the dark of night, making their way weakly across the valley by torchlight, joining the three others in the hut.

When Gray Hawk called a council, I left my children with Hawk Sister and went to the townhouse to hear what was said. Mink told the council that the sick house was full. "We should have built more than one hut," he said. "Tomorrow we shall go to another part of the river and build more."

Then Bender rose to speak. "It seems it is not going so well as our beloved brother in his wisdom had planned," he said, hardly trying now to hide his contempt. "Soon all the town will be freezing to death in flimsy huts by the river. Those the Sun might spare, the Winter will claim. Or perhaps the Coosas will get them first."

Mink stepped again into the firelight, his figure stooped beneath the weight of what he knew. "I was hoping it would not be so bad," he said quietly. "I wanted the fire to strike just a few of us without taking us all. But that is not to be. I do not know how many of us will suffer before it is over. Yet, even if as many as half the people in the town are burned, we must continue to keep the sick apart from the well. We *must* do it, even if we have to put out our *own children* to lie dying on the frozen ground." Mink's face contorted as he spoke. It twisted in an agony I could not watch. I could not bear his pain. I rose from my seat and stumbled out of the townhouse.

The next day more huts were built. There were people waiting to move into them, sick people lying under bearskins on the ground outside the palisade. In all, the fire came to seven on that day. They came from houses all across the village.

On the third day the town was still. At dawn six more made their way to the huts. But there was no more wailing in the town. Fear had brought a silence. The beloved men gathered at the townhouse, but they had little to say. Women on their way to get water met and stood together speaking softly, sometimes hugging one another before they went on their way. The children played—they will always play—but they cried easily over nothing.

In the afternoon we heard a shout, then a commotion at the palisade entrance. I called my children and sent them into the house before going myself to see what was happening. A great many people had gathered, and I moved through until I could see into the open space in their midst. There, looking with challenge at the crowd, were Red Dog and his brother and his brother's wife, the three who had first felt the fire. Instinctively I pulled back. "What are they doing here?" I asked a woman next to me.

"They have survived the fire," she said. "Their fever is gone."

"But they are not scarred."

"Mink is powerful," she said, smiling at me knowingly.

I turned from her and began to look for Mink across the crowd, scanning the faces until I found him. I saw his anger as Bender came forward to escort the three survivors to their homes.

I left and went back to Hawk Sister's house. Mink arrived soon after. "Have they truly recovered?" I asked.

"It seems so," he answered grimly. "But I don't like it. I have not heard of anyone recovering so fast—and without scars."

"Did you ask them not to come back?"

"I tried. But Bender said it would be better for them to return to their homes than to freeze in the hut."

"They would not freeze."

"I know. But the woman is his niece. Bender is like a blind man."

By the next morning, only two more in the town had taken the fever. We began to feel hopeful. After breakfast I took my two children and went across the plaza to visit my mother. Four Paws, her brother, was one of those in the sick huts, but we did not speak of him. We talked quietly together about spring, about the fish that would be running and how good they would taste. We sat together, the two of us, and dreamed of spring, as if none of our friends and relatives were dying in the huts. I cannot explain why we were not grieving. Even my grief for Trotting Wolf was numbed by the strangeness of those days.

In the afternoon, the children and I walked back toward Hawk Sister's house, going slowly so that Little Cougar could keep up. We heard a disturbance at the edge of the plaza, and as we drew near, Traveler ran ahead to see. He would not hear me when I called him back. I picked up Little Cougar and followed, feeling the anger that was in the air. Traveler pushed in through the crowd, as a child can do, but as I tried to go after him, I met a wall of shoulders.

"What is it?" I asked a man in front of me. "What is happening?"

"Red Dog," hissed the man.

"What has he done?"

"Witch. All three of them, witches. They came back to burn us."

"But they were well."

"Trickery," the man spat. "Today their skin is scorched red, burned by the Sun!"

"Witch!" someone yelled, and the crowd moved, pushing forward.

I called Traveler, but I knew he could not hear me. I pushed frantically into the crowd, reaching out with my free hand to make a space to squeeze through. Little Cougar on my hip was pressed and jostled and began to cry. I paid her no mind. I was looking for Traveler, such a small boy to find in an angry mob.

"Witches!" someone screamed, and all at once I could see

the three huddled against the side of a house. As I watched, they broke and ran, heading for the palisade entrance.

"Witches!" cried the people, throwing stones at them as they fled. I turned away, looking for Traveler, and saw Bender hurling a stone at his own niece. "I hope she has *burned* you!" I hissed, ugly, like the rest of the crowd. Then there was a tug at my hand, and I looked down to see Traveler, pale with fear.

"Do not look at them!" I said, sick inside that he was seeing this. With Little Cougar in one arm, I held Traveler tightly by the hand and pulled him along, pushing, fighting against the crowd, until at last we broke free. I ran with them all the way home.

Hawk Sister and Mink were gone, and the fire had died low. I sat down by the hearth and added wood, blowing to bring up a flame. Little Cougar was snuffling in my lap. I wrapped my arms around her to comfort her. "It was nothing," I whispered. "Nothing at all. Do not think about it any more." Traveler sat quietly beside me and leaned his head against me. At last he said, "Are they witches?"

"They are sick," I said, not knowing the answer to his question.

"Do they have a headache?"

"Their skin is burned."

"I have a headache, my mother."

A thud of fear. "Not a bad one," I said, forcing the words to calmness.

"Not bad at first. But it is starting to be."

I reached down and felt his face, but my hand was trembling, my mind jumping. I could not tell. I took a deep breath, trying to calm myself. Absently I stroked Little Cou-

gar, pushing the hair from her face. Then my hand stopped. . . .

I heard a moan from my own lips. Shaking now—I could
not stop the shaking—I pressed my hand against her face and
felt the warmth of the fever, the rising warmth, the slow
burning of the Sun. I felt Traveler's face again. A little
warm, but not so much as she. I felt my own face and it was
cool. I felt his again and it was warm. And hers was warmer
still.

I wanted to scream and run in circles and shake down the
house. I wanted to fight against it. I wanted to pour water on
Ancient Fire and run screaming through the town and pull
down the townhouse and flatten the palisade. But instead I
held my children to me and caressed them, and slowly, slowly
strength flowed into my arms and into my heart.

"We must go away," I said softly.

Traveler was silent, and I wondered if he knew. I wondered if a boy of six years could understand.

I got up and smoothed my skirt. I took a deep breath and
held it, then let it out slowly. I went over and took down a
large burden basket from its hook on the wall. Now, what
would we need? Food. I went to a basket in the corner and
took out a skin sack. Not big enough. I put it back, then
found one that seemed right. I went to the jar that held the
ground parched corn, cold meal for making mush. There was
not much in the jar. I scooped some of it into the bag and
then looked at it and looked back into the jar and thought
about Mink and Hawk Sister. I should leave some for them. I
started to tie the bag. Then I stopped. I looked at the jar
again. Then I opened the bag and filled it with the rest of the
cold meal. They would want me to have it. I hoped they
would. I tied up the bag and put it in the bottom of the

burden basket. Then I took another sack and filled it with dried beans. There were plenty of beans. Beans and cold meal—it would hold us.

What else would we need? I picked up a knife and threw it in. And spoons. I put in a large stirring spoon and two small ones. A pot! Of course—a pot for cooking. And water jars. How could I carry so much? Gourds. I should use gourd bottles for water. An axe. And blankets—warm skins against the winter cold.

The burden basket was filled. Surely it was not all I needed. But it was all I could carry. It was enough. Then I thought for a moment and put in some fishhooks and a fishing spear and Traveler's blowgun. I looked at Mink's bow hanging on the wall by the door. I took it with his quiver of arrows and propped them against the basket.

We dressed ourselves warmly, putting on more than we needed so that we would have extra clothing. Then I slung the bow and quiver across my back. I stooped and placed the burden strap against my forehead and rose with the basket on my back, bracing my neck and shoulders against the weight.

"What shall I carry, my mother?" asked Traveler.

"Nothing, my son. Just bring yourself."

Then I remembered fire. How could I have forgotten it? "We need fire, my son. You can bring the fire."

Traveler went to the hearth and took up one of the clay pots there, a small pot tied around with a leather strap. He put in some coals from the fire and covered them with ashes. Then he took it up by the leather strap, and we were ready.

"Take your sister's hand," I said, and then, like a hollow dream, I led them out into the town and headed for the palisade entrance. I walked as quickly as I could, my eyes on the ground, not wanting to see anyone, not wanting to be seen.

"Shall we tell our grandmother we are going?" asked Little Cougar.

I wondered at the trust of children, that they had not yet even asked where we were going—or why. "No," I said. "Hawk Sister will tell her for us."

We walked around the edge of the plaza, staying in the shadows of the houses. People must have seen us, shaken their heads sadly, and looked away. But I did not see them. I watched the ground and strained against the weight of the basket.

"Rain Dove!" I flinched when I heard my name called and tears sprang to my eyes.

"Run, my children!" I began to push with my legs, trying to run, trying to get away from Mink.

"Rain Dove." His voice stopped me, the tenderness of it, the fullness. I turned to face him, pushing my children behind me. I let down the burden basket.

"Do not come near," I said. "It has come to my children."

Ignoring my warning, Mink came to me and stood close, looking into my face, his eyes reaching into me. It was agony to behold the sorrow in his face. Since summer he had lived a hundred years.

"They will have to leave the town," he said, almost without voice.

"I know," I said softly. "You can see that they are going."

"Whoever nurses them will also suffer from the fire."

"They are my children."

Tears came to his eyes, but he caught them. Then he forced a smile as he looked at the bow across my back. "Can you shoot a man's bow?"

"I doubt it," I murmured, attempting a little laugh. "But I might try if I have to."

"You must go to the cove," he said, strong again, in charge.

"The cove? I thought the huts. . . ."

"There are going to be too many there. They will run out of food—and wood. The valley is scoured clean of wood—you know that. It is going to be a terrible time ahead. You'll not be able to depend on people. They will be as sick and cold and hungry as you are. They'll fight for the last root to eat and for every twig that falls from the trees. You would do better in the cove. It will be warmer there in the shelter of the rocks. And there will be wood—no one has ever gathered there. And no one will fight you for your food."

"But all alone? I cannot do that."

"Yes you can. Build a sweat lodge big enough to hold the three of you. Gather as much firewood as you can, and bring in as much water as possible. When the sickness strikes you, you will not be able to care for yourself. So do what you can beforehand. Gather willow bark to use against the fever. And try to find some spikenard and snakeroot. Brew it all together. Mostly it should be drunk, but some of it you can spray with your mouth on the burning skin. At least once a day you should sweat the children and dip them in running water. And make them eat. Their mouths and throats will be sore, and they will not want to eat, but if they don't they will die. But don't spoil the medicines and sweatings with food. Feed them after the treatments. And you, when you are sick, you must be sure to eat. It will keep you strong. Promise me you will eat, little wren."

"I promise," I whispered, tears blurring against my eyes.

He took from around his neck the shell pendant he wore, a round disk with serpent dancers carved upon it. As he slipped it over my head, he pressed his hands hard against my shoulders. "There is power in it," he said softly. "I will be working for you every day, singing songs for you when I plunge into the river."

I nodded, and stooping for the burden strap, I rose with the basket on my back. Then I turned and walked away, leading my children from the town. I looked back once and saw Mink watching. After that I did not look again.

"Where is the cove?" asked Traveler as we followed the path through the dried cornfields in the valley.

"Up the river, in the hills. It's a pretty place. You will like it."

"Carry me," said Little Cougar. "I'm too tired."

"I've so much to carry, little daughter. Try to walk. We'll soon be there."

She walked as far as the river, but as we turned up the trail there, she sat down on the ground and began to cry. I felt her face. It was burning. I took her up in my arms and we pushed ahead, stopping often to rest, sweating in the cold of winter, she from the fever, I from my burdens.

"How is it with you, my son?" I kept asking Traveler.

"I am fine," he would reply. But each time I felt his face, he was warmer. Before we reached the cove, he too was sweating, though his breath blew cold and frosty in the air.

On the floor of the cove I spread a bearskin and laid Little Cougar upon it. Traveler dropped down beside her. I smiled and kissed him. "You were a strong one to walk all the way."

"I don't feel so well," he said.

"I know. I will build a sweat lodge and gather some medicines. Mink has told me just what to do to make you better."

"Are we witches?"

"No, my little son. Your hearts are white."

"Then why did we have to come here?"

"Because it is the best place for getting well."

He looked up beyond me to the treetops, some of them bare, some green with needles. The sky beyond was clear, winter blue. "It's pretty here," he said. "But it's cold." He shivered, the sweat of fever running on his face.

I folded the bearskin over the two of them. "I will be back," I said. "I have to gather what I need for the lodge."

I know now why there are omens. I know a thing can be so horrible that the world must shudder at its coming. I could not have dreamed a thing so terrible as the burning sickness, not in my blackest nightmares. Nothing like it had ever been before upon the earth.

I built a lodge, a very small lodge of bent poles covered with layer after layer of thick cedar boughs. I built it right beside the stream, so that I could almost reach the water from the doorway. As I worked, my children tossed with fever, groaning with aching heads and backs. As soon as I finished the lodge and had gathered some wood, I sweated them and dipped them in the cold running water of the stream. Then I left them sleeping in the lodge, warm by the fire, and I went out to gather more wood. I walked around through the forest until I knew every part of it, and as I gathered wood, I looked for medicine. I stacked the wood high by the door and boiled more medicine than I needed for the children.

After two days their fevers broke, and they seemed all at once to be getting well. But I remembered Red Dog, how his fever had broken and he had come back to the town. I knew it was not a hopeful sign. Yet it was a chance to talk with them and laugh. I will remember always the way they were that day. I try to remember it above the rest.

Then, in the night the burning erupted on their bodies. In

the light of dawn I saw redness on their faces, on their arms and hands, and on their feet, as if the sun had burned them. Through the day the redness spread across their bodies. I sweated them and dipped them in the stream and gave them medicine to drink. I spewed more medicine upon their skin.

In the days that followed, the burned skin began to blister. It itched and burned, and when they scratched, the blisters would break open and run and bleed. I sweated them and dipped them in the stream and tried to feed them a thin corn gruel. And I sat with them, talking to them, trying to keep them from scratching. Whenever they slept, I hurried out to gather wood, and I filled the water gourds to the very top, for I did not know how long it would be before the fever came also to me.

As terrible as it was to watch my children suffer, it was even worse to watch alone, without another living soul to comfort me and turn my mind to easier things. When the blisters became fetid and began to smell of death, when a new fever burst upon them, when their skin became so swollen that I could hardly recognize them as my own, then I needed very much not to be alone. I needed help against a growing madness.

I sat for hours and stared at them, watched them toss in the delirium of the fever. And I thought about the strangers. Where had they come from? Why had they come to our shore and wronged the Chicoras, who had never done any hurtful thing to them? Why had they come, only to go and leave my children suffering so? My people had no stories that told of such a thing as this. There was nothing in our knowledge to give me comfort or to help me understand. And so I sat and stared at my children and wrung my hands like a mad person.

Little Cougar died of the fever and my thoughts stopped. My soul lifted from my body and left the hut. Cold and black, I sat beside the fire and stared at my little daughter dead before me. How would it end? There would be no kinsmen to wail and bury us. The wolves would find us and scatter our bones.

I carried Little Cougar out of the hut and laid her beside the stream, and I wailed over her there, softly so that Traveler could not hear. My soul had gone out of me and left me cold. No longer fighting death, I turned to it, stretching out my hand.

But the wolves would not have our bones. I would see to that. I made a death house for us, a small place, just big enough for the three of us. I used stones to build up the sides. I laid Little Cougar inside it and covered her with cedar boughs. For a roof I pulled the sheets of loose bark from a lightning-struck tree and laid the bark across the stones, using more stones to hold it in place against the wolves. When Traveler died, I would put him in it. And when my own time came and my strength was all but gone, I would take the stones from one end and crawl inside and build the wall up after me. Then someday someone would find our bones and give us a decent burial in the earth.

I went back to Traveler, to tend to the living. But I no longer tried to gather wood or keep the gourds all filled with water. Everything seemed hopeless now. A numbness grew, and the world began to blur, became dreamlike. I lay beside Traveler and talked to him, moving only to add more wood to the fire or to pour water and gruel down my son's burning throat. Sometimes he would choke and cry out, and I would drop the water bottle and cover my ears and rock back and forth, moaning and weeping. But the dullness in my mind had become my comfort, and soon I would be lying next to him again, talking to him. I was telling him about my life, telling everything that had ever happened to me from as early as I could remember. I was careful to point out the lessons, whenever there were lessons to be learned. These are things a mother should tell a child. Sometimes he turned and looked at me, but I do not think he was listening.

All time ran together—days and nights. I cannot remember when the fever struck me. I only remember trying to rise, knowing that I should not let the fire go out. It was as if someone were sitting on me, a great, heavy weight, as I struggled up onto my elbows and then collapsed. I lay panting, thinking of death. And suddenly I wanted to live. Even without my children, without Trotting Wolf, without my brothers, without any who were ever dear to me—I still wanted my life.

The hut was small; it was not far to the fire. I tried again, struggling until I had pulled myself to it and added wood to the coals. Then I moved to Traveler and gave him water. I drank some myself and felt it burn my throat as it went down. I moved my place closer to the fire and pulled Traveler next to me and put the water and the wood where I could reach them. Then I lay back and slept.

In time the fever broke. Now I would have a little while before the burning broke out on my skin. I was weak, but I could get around, and I went out and gathered wood and stacked it high beside the fire. I filled the gourd bottles and set them in reach. Making up some mush, I thinned it almost to water and fed it to Traveler. It was a wonder to me that he was yet alive. His fever had fallen and in places the sores on his skin were drying up. But the skin was so terribly injured. It smelled of death. He lay still and quiet.

I soon felt an itching on my forehead. I reached up but felt nothing. Then I looked at my hands and saw the redness. It spread quickly to every part of me. After a day I could feel the little bumps rising. My mouth and my throat became so sore that I no longer wanted to eat. But I had promised Mink. For him I would eat, no matter what the pain.

I was thinking often now of Mink. If only he could be here taking care of us. Maybe he would come. He knew where we were. Only he knew. This was his cove—our cove. Could he let me lie here alone, burning with fever? He would come. I knew that Mink would come.

I began to tell Traveler he was coming. As I poured the gruel down his throat, I would say to him, "Don't worry, my little son. Mink will soon be here. He will give you medicine to heal your throat." Then I would lie beside him and listen. I was always listening now for the sound of Mink coming up the trail. I knew that he was coming. The second fever would soon be upon me, and it would be worse than the first. If there was no one to help me, I would die. Mink had to come. He had to know that I needed him. I waited for him, always listening.

I do not know how long it was, how many days, but at last I felt the second fever rising. And Mink had not yet come. It was painful to move, for the sores were even on the bottoms of my feet and on the palms of my hands and on my knees. But still I moved around and set things up as well as I was able. I piled as much wood as I could onto the coals of the fire, stacking it as tightly as possible, covering it with ashes, leaving little room for air so that it would burn low without flaming up all at once. I filled all the gourd bottles with the thin gruel Traveler and I had been drinking, and I took half of the bottles and set them beside him, well within his reach.

"My little son," I said to him. "Can you hear me? Here are the bottles of gruel. You can reach them here. If you get too thirsty before I can help you drink, then you must drink by yourself . . . until Mink comes to help us." I did not really think Traveler would be able to drink by himself, but it was all I could do.

The fever was taking me. I lay down weakly, placing the rest of the gruel within my own reach. I would keep my promise to Mink and drink it as long as I could get it to my mouth. He would be pleased when he arrived and saw that we had been eating. I was listening for him, waiting to hear him coming up the path.

Perhaps I slept a little before I heard my name. Perhaps I was sleeping, for it startled me, and I felt it was not the first time I had been called.

"I am here!" I answered, but the words hardly came out. I reached for the gruel and dribbled a little down my throat. Then I said again, "I am here!" and though hoarse and rasping, my voice was loud enough to be heard.

"Mink sent me," said the voice outside the hut. My heart fell that it was not Mink himself.

"Tell him I need him," I said, but the words were too feeble to be understood. I took another drink of gruel, a very small drink. My head was swimming with fever.

"He asked me to tell you this," said the man. I did not recognize the voice. Whoever it was, I began to realize that he was not coming in. I wished so much that he would, that I could look once more upon a human face. But I knew he was right to stay outside. So I lay quietly and listened.

"He asked me to tell you about the town. It is filled with death. There are too many sick now for the huts to be of use, and every day another house is struck. There are not even half of us left who have not been burned. Mink said that we should leave. All who have not been burned are leaving. We are going into the mountains to a place known only to those leading us. It is Mink's idea that we should hide ourselves, that we should not have contact with any other people until the fire has gone from the land. No one must come to us, and no one must go out from us. Even you who are left behind are not to know where we are. When we are sure the fire is gone, we will come back and get you."

It was hard for me to listen to him. I could not imagine the town abandoned. I was already so alone in the cove. And now, in the valley below, the town would be empty, filled only with the ghosts of the dead.

"Mink said that you should keep eating. He said the food will give strength to your body. He said that I should tell you that."

"Tell Mink it is for him I keep eating." My voice rasped and tore at my throat.

"Mink is dead," said the messenger.

"Mink is dead," I whispered. I clutched at the blanket beneath me and turned my face against it, losing myself in painful sobbing. There was nothing left. My husband was dead, my two brothers, my little daughter. My son was dying. And now Mink was dead. I was dead, too. There was nothing left of me.

I gave the messenger no answer, nothing to let him know that I had heard. I do not know how long it was before he left. I do not know if he spoke any more to me. Mink was dead. I knew nothing else. The fever pulled at me. I let go and sank into the spin of it.

Time was lost. I was whirling, turning, dropping through empty space, falling from the heavens. A river rushed up and caught me. I was floating now, caught in the current of the river, pulled under by the freezing waters. So cold. I was shaking from the cold. I was drowning.

But the river would not take me. It washed me up, threw me onto the sand. The summer sun beat down, blistering hot, sweat pouring, sand clinging, rubbing raw into my skin. I lay for days in the sun, for months, it seemed, aching and burning. Oh, the river. To feel it again. To have it wash over me and cool me. . . . In spring the waters would rise and wash over me. . . . If only I could live until spring. If only I could.

Time passed unmeasured, days on end of scorching heat. So much burning of the sun. Oh, for the River. The River. To feel it again. . . .

But what was this? The River! I had lived to feel the waters. The coolness, the soothing wetness. It washed over me. I could feel it on my arms and legs, and on my face. I felt it flowing over my face, washing against my eyes and into my mouth. I choked. I raised a little and coughed, choking on the water.

"I am sorry, my mother. I didn't mean to choke you."

"Traveler?" I whispered. I opened my eyes and looked at him in confusion. How could this be? This poor thing—was he really my son? This thin, scab-covered, mangy-haired little creature? He was smiling at me. He was beautiful. He had lived through the fire.

"You asked for the river," he said. His voice was hoarse, but it was strong enough. "I tried, but I could not take you to it. So I am bringing it in bottles."

I smiled, not taking my eyes from him. "It feels so good," I whispered. "Now can you help me drink some gruel? Mink said that we must eat."

TEN

Traveler, born with the power of a younger twin, had not yet acquired knowledge, for he was too young to have had a teacher. But even without knowledge, he had the touch of a healer and the wisdom of one who could see. He told me that we would not die. As he fed me gruel and washed my hurt skin with cold river water, he told me that he had seen that we would live, that in a dream he had seen the two of us walking through the river valley outside the town.

But if we were to live, it was not to be without a struggle. Surviving the fever was but the first ordeal. I lay helpless and saw how slowly Traveler moved about the hut, how his strength seemed unwilling to return. Very soon we would need firewood and food. I worried that we had survived the fever only to starve to death or freeze in the late winter cold.

"As soon as you are strong enough, you should look for firewood," I told him. "Perhaps you can find some nearby."

"Are we going to stay here much longer, my mother?"

"Until we are well enough to go back to the valley."

"What if no one is there?"

"There will be someone there. We'll wait with them until we hear from the new town. Then we'll go wherever the town has moved. Higher up in the mountains, I think. Would you like to live in the high mountains?"

"What if we wait in the valley and the new town doesn't send for us?"

"They will."

"But if they don't, what will we do? Live all alone?"

"They will send for us. They are our kinsmen."

"But they might think we are dead. What would we do then? They would not send for us if they thought we were dead."

"Someone is driving his mother crazy with too many questions. What if the sky falls down on you? Then what would you do?"

"Swim."

"Swim?" I looked at him and started to laugh.

"Like a frog," he giggled and began to swim around the hut, kicking out his legs like a frog.

By the time I could sit up and move about a little inside the hut, Traveler was able to walk around the cove; but more than that was too much for him. I worried about firewood and wished that in the beginning I had not picked up all that was near the camp, that I had brought it from farther away. I should have thought of this.

"What about the old log?" I asked Traveler. The log Mink and I used to sit on. Pain at the sudden memory.

"It is too big."

"But it is rotten, my son. Take the axe and see if you can knock off a piece of it."

He took the axe and went outside and I heard him chopping at the log. Then he was back again in the doorway, holding a piece of black, mossy wood. "It works," he said.

"And it's a good thing, because I think a storm is coming."

I moved to the doorway and looked out. The sky was gray, hanging low with flat, unbroken clouds. A winter storm. I took the wood from Traveler and put it near the fire to dry. "At least we will be warm," I said. "Can you bring more?"

He worked until dark, using up more strength and energy than he had. Then he fell exhausted on the bearskin by the fire and looked with satisfaction at our pile of wood. It would take us through the storm. But to myself I wondered what we would do after that.

The storm began in the night. I listened to it, cold rain turning to sleet; snow would follow, but I slept before it came. Long after dawn I awoke. It was cold. In the hearth a few small coals were scattered among the ashes. I raked them together and added wood, rotten wood that burned away quickly, leaving scarcely any coals to hold the heat. Then suddenly I realized what I was hearing in the storm; not the silence of snowfall, but rain, still raining—or sleeting. I hurried to the doorway, pushed away the boughs, and looked out.

"An ice storm, my son! It's not snow—it's ice! The dead limbs will break from the trees. We'll have wood!" But Traveler was sleeping and did not hear me. So exhausted from the day before, he did not awaken until evening.

In midafternoon the sleet stopped. As the sun came out, it grew colder. From the doorway of the hut I looked out on a shimmering world of ice, frozen and silent. Evergreens drooped gracefully with the weight of their branches, every needle and twig encased in ice, clear as sparkling water. It was beautiful. Too beautiful. Such loveliness did not belong anymore. Things had become too sad, too pitiful. I looked at Little Cougar's tomb of stone and bark, covered with icicles, stark against the changed landscape. And tears came, I could not hold them back. Too much aching in my heart. I wanted to be strong again. I wanted to go back to the valley and find what was left. I wanted to live again among people.

But I was too weak to go. And tears would not make me stronger. Wiping them away, I felt the rough scabs on my face, and I nearly wept again. How strange that this was as hard to bear as any of it: I did not want to be scarred and ugly.

I was not alone in that. Not many days after, I found Traveler looking at my face, feeling with his hand the scars on his own. He knew what it meant. He had seen the young men of the town preening themselves in their yards, then strutting handsomely about the plaza. He was old enough to know that he did not want to be ugly. But he did not speak of it. When he saw me looking, he dropped his hand.

"Tell me, my son," I said to him. "What is the most beautiful thing you can think of?"

"What do you mean?"

"Name something so beautiful that it takes your breath away when you think of it."

"My breath away?"

"Like this." And I gasped for him, wide-eyed, as if I had just seen something marvelous.

"The most beautiful thing was going into the mountains with Two Crows to see the golden eagles."

"What was beautiful, the eagles or the mountains?"

"The eagles . . . *and* the mountains. All of it."

"Then what if I call you Mountain Eagle? Will you think yourself handsome if I call you that?"

Traveler smiled. "It's a nice name."

"A handsome name," I said. "A handsome name for a handsome boy."

His hand went again to his face. But he was still smiling. "You should have a name, too," he said. "You have scars like me."

"Yes, I could use a pretty name. Like the sea at dawn. I've never seen it, but I have always heard there is nothing more beautiful. If you call me Sea Dawn, I will feel very lovely. As long as we stay here in the cove, you will be Mountain Eagle and I will be Sea Dawn."

"And let's pretend that we were captured by enemies," said Traveler. "I'm a warrior and you can be my mother. We were taken from our town to Coosa country, but now we have escaped. You've been sick, and I'm taking care of you while we make our way back home."

"And I am getting better," I added, marveling that in the midst of all that was happening, he was still a child.

As our mouths and throats healed, our appetites returned, Traveler's first, then mine. We were wasted from the sickness, thin and hollow-cheeked. Almost before I knew it, the cold meal was gone and the beans were running out. I kept our portions small, but it was difficult, for we were hungry and could have eaten twice or three times our ration.

It was not that there was no food in the forest. We were too weak to gather it. But though we lacked endurance to wander, we could wait. And so we built traps. We first made traps in the stream. I told Traveler how to make a rock trap, how to pile stones across the channel in a V-shape to guide the fish to the open point on the downstream side. At the point we attached a basket trap that I made with split cane, and we sat back and watched it, sure that everything that swam downstream would end up in our bellies. But it was not a foolproof trap. There were gaps between the rocks that small fish could swim through, and often the basket would tip or tear loose on one side. Once it washed away completely and I had to weave another. We got a few fish from the trap, but not enough. We were hungry.

I plaited cord for snare traps, but I did not have the fibers I needed to make good ones. We caught one small possum. Other creatures that sprang the traps got away because the cord was too stiff to pull tightly around them. And nothing ventured near the deadfall traps we set up. The small amount of plant food near our cove was soon gone, a few roots and some tender cane shoots. I found myself eyeing the bark on the trees, remembering starvation stories I had heard. How long before we came to that?

"We are going on an expedition," I said to Traveler. "A food-gathering expedition."

It is hard now to imagine how weak we were. I could not walk a stone's throw without sitting down to rest. And digging roots was even harder. We worked from dawn until sundown, though at least half of that time we were resting. It was exhilarating to find a patch of wild onions: green food and a promise of spring. But it was Traveler who made it such an important day. He was the one who found the deer tracks.

"A deer has been here to drink," he said. I was sitting on a rock to rest, and he was poking around the stream. "If I were a man, I would kill it."

I got up slowly and went over to look. There were tracks from several different days, or so it seemed.

"I think this deer has been here more than once," said Traveler.

"Perhaps so," I replied, and I sat down to think.

The next afternoon I returned to the spot with Mink's bow. I left Traveler alone at the camp, telling him I might not return until the next day. And I tried to tell him how unlikely it was that I would actually be able to kill the deer. He began to understand this when he saw how I struggled to string the bow.

"It takes strength to kill a deer," I said, "and I do not have it." He nodded. "I will try," I added, "but I don't want you disappointed when I come back with nothing." Yet I think he was tasting the deer meat as I left. I told him to call if he needed me, for the place with the deer tracks was not so very far away.

I had a plan, but I knew all along how terribly difficult it would be. I would hide in the laurel close beside the spot where the deer had stood to drink, so close that even with my weak pull on the bow, the arrow might have enough force to kill. If I only wounded the deer, I knew I would not have the strength to follow it. So I had another plan, one I realized was too crazy to be of use. Before the deer had a chance to run, I thought, I would leap out and finish it off with my knife. I knew it could not be done, but I was ready to try anything. I was starving.

I had hoped the deer would come at dusk. I did not like the idea of crouching in the laurel through the night; and I worried about Traveler, all alone, afraid in the hut. But the light faded and stars came out, and there was no sign of the deer. That was when it first occurred to me that the deer might not come at all. I had assumed it would return to this particular spot at the stream and that it would come while I was waiting in the laurel. But now that it was dark and cold and I was stiff from crouching for so long, I began to think that maybe it would be best to give it up and return to camp. But I was hungry. And there was no food in the camp. So I stayed in the laurel and waited into the night.

I tried to hold the position I would shoot from, silent and unmoving, keeping an arrow nocked in the bow. The waiting was terrible. I could hardly bear it. Only the thought of Traveler kept me there. I would think about how thin he was, how weak, how he would waste away and die unless I found food for him. I stayed and waited, aching in every part of my body, weak and cold, dozing, jerking awake to peer out anxiously into the moonlight, fearful that the deer had come and gone while I had slept.

At dawn, I watched the light rise in the forest. Shadows fell away. A bird, perhaps warmed by the sun, began to sing. And I knew that the awful night had been for nothing. There would be no deer. No meat in our camp. We would starve, too weak to ever make our way down to the valley.

Then suddenly the deer was there. It stepped in front of me to the stream's edge. A buck. A large, beautiful buck. I froze, my hands trembling on the bow. For a moment the buck stood still, looking for danger. Then he lowered his head and began to drink. So much meat on that animal. So much food. Aim for the chest! For the heart! Suddenly I was pulling back the bow, back and back, as far as a man would pull it, and an arrow was flying, burying itself deep in the deer. He bolted forward, then doubled up as he fell face down in the stream. For a time his legs kicked. Then all was still. I stumbled out of the laurel, trembling and unbelieving. Too weak to stand, I knelt beside the slain animal and whispered the song of thanks to the White Deer Spirit.

Traveler was happy to be going home, happier than I, now that the time had come. The two months since we left seemed like years. Everything we had left behind would be changed, people dead, nothing as we had known it. I tried to tell him that, but he would not hear me, not until we came out from the trees along the river and stood looking about the valley. All was still and eerie. No one on the paths. No guards on the palisade. No smoke. No fires in the town. No people.

"No one is here," whispered Traveler. I thought he was going to cry.

"There must be some people somewhere," I said. But I too was truly afraid that we were all alone, that no one else was left.

"Shall we look in the town?" he asked.

"No!"

He looked up at me in surprise.

"A great many people have died," I explained again gently. He nodded. He knew, but only now was he beginning to understand. "People that we know have died. Your sister. Mink. And others, though we don't yet know who. We don't know how many. But now that we are down here, we will be finding out. No one is in the town because so many died there. It belongs now to the dead. There is no one in there who can tell us anything."

"Then where is everyone?"

"They are somewhere. We will find them."

I had brought down our things in the burden basket, and now as we moved back toward the river, I left the basket leaning against a tree. I would come back for it after we had found the people. "We'll look this way first," I said, pointing down the river trail.

I took his hand as we set out. Along the way I showed him signs of spring—swelling buds and early green plants, robins and bluebirds. "It all turns in a circle," I told him. "There will always be spring."

I saw the sick huts ahead, no smoke above them, abandoned.

"Is that where they are living?" asked Traveler.

"No. People were sick in those, like we were sick in the cove."

As we hurried past them, Traveler tried to look inside. "Are there dead people in there?" he said.

"I don't know, my son. You shouldn't look."

Beyond them, I slowed again and then stopped to show him some new little ferns, tightly coiled, pushing up from the earth.

"You there!" called a voice.

I whirled and looked back toward the sick huts. On the path was an old woman, strong of step as she came toward us. And behind her a girl, young breasts disfigured by scars. I stared at the old woman, and she at me, each of us changed and strange to the other. Then she knew me, her face breaking into a smile, and in her smile I recognized Full Moon Woman, the old midwife who had helped me give birth to my children. I wanted to weep as she embraced me, but I had had too much weeping. I squeezed shut my eyes and hugged her, for a long time clinging to her, so glad that there was someone else, so glad not to be alone anymore.

She motioned us down and we sat together, the four of us, among the new spring ferns. The girl I recognized as Deerfoot, a daughter of Full Moon Woman's clan. I asked if they lived in one of the huts we had passed.

"No," said Full Moon Woman. "Those belong to the dead."

"Then why did you sneak up behind us?" asked Traveler.

We looked at him and laughed, making him drop his eyes in embarrassment.

"We did not mean to sneak," said Full Moon Woman. "We saw your pack basket near the trail, and we were trying to catch up to see who you were."

"Where are you living?" I asked her. "Here in the valley?"

"The valley did not seem a good place for us anymore. We are living at the ball ground. There are about thirty of us. That is all that is left."

Only thirty. I could not bear to ask who they were. "Has there been word from the new town?"

"Nothing," she said. There was a silence, and then she got to her feet. "We will go back for your basket. You can live with us in our house."

There were eight houses at the ball ground. Not good houses. No one was strong enough to build a good house. But all the houses were better than the little hut of cedar boughs that Traveler and I had left behind. They were in a circle, all facing onto a central yard. There were cookfires in the yard, and a few tanning frames, and even dogs. It surprised me to see dogs. Perhaps because they made things seem so normal.

Everyone came out into the yard as we arrived. I felt ashamed at how I looked. But each of them was also disfigured. I was hoping to find Hawk Sister, but she was not there. Nor were my mother and my father. But I saw Rising Moon, the widow of my brother Two Crows, and she had her oldest child and also Little Buck's child. I knew then that Little Buck's wife was dead. But Fawn was there, my father's niece. And Four Paws, my beloved uncle. Those were the only ones who had been close to me before the sickness came. But I recognized all the others, and they welcomed me with gladness and drew me into their circle.

Four Paws was headman here, the only man left with such experience in leadership. In the old days he had been the headman of the Bird clan. He was living now in the house next to Full Moon Woman. His wife's brother and a grandson of his wife's clan lived with him. Fawn lived in the next house with a clan sister and an uncle and a little girl of their lineage. Rising Moon had a house with her father and the two children. In another house was Red Dog, the hunter who had first felt the fire and had been driven from Mulberry Town as a witch. His wife was there, too, and I looked at them with envy, wishing that it were Trotting Wolf and I who were standing here together.

Full Moon Woman welcomed Traveler and me into her house. She lived there with the girl Deerfoot. I could see that they had tried to make it a cheerful place. Full Moon Woman at once became my comfort, strong and steady, taking charge. The old woman knew things—I quickly felt it—she could see the world from the center. I let myself go, falling into her care, seeking rest in her like a child in its mother's arms.

We sat late by the fire that first night, drinking tea she had made. I wanted to ask about people, to find out what had happened. I waited first for Traveler and Deerfoot to fall asleep. And even after that I waited, afraid to open the questions, afraid of what I would hear. But at last I knew I had to speak. "Tell me, my grandmother," I said softly. "Do you know about Hawk Sister?"

For a long time Full Moon Woman was silent. Then she said, "Yes, my child. She died of the fever. It took her right away, even before any burning appeared on her skin. A few lucky ones died that way, still with their beauty. With her I think it was more than the fever. There was that other illness that had been growing in her."

I stared into the fire, feeling no shock, no sudden sadness. There was only that ache that was so deep, the ache that had now been there so long. I knew already that almost everyone was dead. The only shock was in finding someone still alive. "Was she buried?" I asked.

"Mink buried her. Beneath the hearth in her house."

My throat thickened at Mink's name. I swallowed, staring into the fire. "I must know how he died," I murmured. I was afraid of what I might hear, afraid that Bender had turned the people against him, that they had killed him.

"He died of the fire," said Full Moon Woman. "Soon after Hawk Sister. He was too weak to survive it very long. He had no one to tend to him, no family. But Gray Hawk would not have him die alone. He took care of Mink himself, sitting beside him until the end. At least, that is what I heard."

"Then it must have been Gray Hawk who came and told me that the town was moving. Mink asked him to."

"Perhaps it was. Gray Hawk did not leave with the town. He had already been struck with the fever. He died of it."

I sighed. Who had not died? "My mother and my father are dead," I said. It was not even a question.

"Yes," said the old woman. "Four Paws told me that they died of the fire."

"And Crazy Eyes, my grandfather."

"Yes. And they say that Running By would not let the old man die alone. They say he stayed with his grandfather and took care of him. Then the fever came to Running By and he died."

I would not have thought that of him. For a moment I was silent. Then I said heavily, "Was anyone left? Who went with the town?"

"None of us knows for sure. We stayed apart from the living. We know only of those who died around us. There were others who died alone, their bones scattered by the dogs. And some of those who started out with the town must have fallen with the fever along the way. So who knows who is left? There were some among us who survived the sickness but wandered away in search of food. They wandered away and never returned. Probably they are dead now. But who can blame them for leaving? There was not enough wood where we were. Not enough food. Those of us who survived saw terrible things. You can see why we did not build these houses in the valley. It was full of death."

I closed my eyes and rested my face in my hands, trying not to think.

"But here at the ball ground it is different," Full Moon Woman said gently, laying a hand on my arm. "This circle of houses is full of life. We are not looking back. When the new town sends for us, we will join them. We will start again. I can remember when Mulberry Town was built up from the ground. In the beginning there was nothing in the valley but grass and trees. I was just a little girl, but I remember it. It was a new start for us, in a new place. I may be old now, but I am ready to start again. And you—you are still young. You have all your life ahead of you."

I shook my head. "It is behind me, my grandmother."

"The other one is. This is a new one that is starting. Look at me, my child. Look how old I am. I have lost more than you—children, grandchildren—I'll not tell you how many. Look at me. Look at how old a woman can be starting over. You are a baby, my child. Just a baby—" Her voice trailed away, her eyes falling shut, and she began to sing, soft and low, a lullaby, gently rocking. Her hand reached out as I moved to her, as I laid my head in her lap, eyes closed, the stroke of her hand on my hair, the loving song, gentle rocking. Not since I was a little girl—not since that faraway time before the omens—had I ever felt such peace. It had come back to me in a circle.

Spring came to the ball ground. A season of healing, of green grass and birdsong and warm days. Enough seed corn had been saved to plant a small plot for the New Corn Festival. There would not be enough for the winter, though, and we worried a little about it. But we were hoping that there was plenty of seed at the new town—and enough people there to plant it. We were expecting any day to see a messenger coming down the path to summon us. We were ready to start again in a new place.

In the meantime we built better houses at the ball ground. We built them in the same place, arranged around the single yard as if we were one family. The women cooked together on fires in the center of the yard, and at night we all sat in one circle beneath the sky, taking turns telling stories of long ago times. The children, playing in the early evening, running in and out of the circle, would gradually settle down to listen and fall asleep one by one in the arms of a father or an aunt or a grandparent. Between tales there were pleasant lulls in which we listened to the night, to the spring peepers singing, to the rustle of soft breezes that filled the air with the scent of green things growing. One night we heard the first of the whippoorwills, returning as they always will for the warm season. We smiled as we heard it, and for a long time we sat silent, listening to that familiar song as to the voice of an old friend.

The days were a mixture of blue skies and spring rains, of warm sun and gusty winds. The earth offered up the most delicate of her foods: the tender wild greens, the sprouting ferns, the mild-fleshed fish, the sweet strawberries. There were pleasant days for gathering, and there was no fear of enemies. The Coosas had turned the balance in their favor the year before and had no reason now to come against us.

I often went out alone to gather food, walking peacefully through the green meadows beneath the sun or through cool shadows of the newly leafed forest.

When most of the strawberries had been picked around the ball ground, I wandered one day along the river below, looking for good patches with fruit that was plump and sweet. The best strawberries seemed to grow beneath the blackberry brambles, lovely now with white blossoms, but as thorny and painful as ever when I reached through them for the strawberries. It would take a long time to fill a basket. I stood up and looked around for another spot. A place without briars would be better.

That was when I saw the four men coming up the trail. It shocked me. Who could this be that was coming? Were they the messengers from the new town? But they were coming from the south. We had thought the town had moved north into the mountains. But they *must* be the messengers. I started toward them and in my excitement began to run. Then suddenly I stopped, my legs almost buckling beneath me. I think I cried out. I do not remember. I remember only seeing Trotting Wolf, seeing him standing still and staring at me with eyes of disbelief. I did not see the scars on his face from the sickness. I did not even see my brother Little Buck standing beside him. I saw only my husband's eyes, nothing more. Then I was in the midst of them and he was holding on to me. And I saw my brother. I turned to embrace him and began to weep. Then all of us were weeping, as people do when they meet after so long a time, when they remember all the people they loved in common who have died since they last parted.

But soon we dried our tears and opened our hearts to joy. I told them about our settlement at the ball ground, and we set out for it at once. As we walked along Trotting Wolf reached out often to touch my cheek, to reassure himself that it was truly I who walked beside him. As for me, I took it all to be a dream and braced myself against the disappointment of awakening, until at last, seeing that it went on too long for a dream, I surrendered to happiness.

That night Little Buck told their story. Trotting Wolf would not tell it. Little Buck told how they had struck the Coosas, how they had been victorious. But they were chased and they circled around and went into the Lower River country, intending to come home that way. On the Lower River they found chaos and sickness. And they themselves fell victim to the burning fire. More than half of them died from the fever, and of those who survived, half again were too weak to live through the hard, hungry winter. When spring came there were only four. These four. One of them my husband. And one my brother.

This was enough for me. I could have lived content forever at the ball ground. But in late spring a runner came at last from the new town and told us there were forty kinsmen there, waiting for us. We eagerly packed our things and followed him north into the mountains, leaving empty our little settlement at the ball ground.

ELEVEN

Ten springs had passed since that spring. Ten seasons of strawberries, and still the best ones grow beneath the brambles. I gather berries now near Quail Town, in our little valley in the high mountains. We call it Quail Town, just as the old town was called in the beginning. It is easy to see how everything moves in a circle. I have seen it many times and cannot doubt that it is true.

If only Traveler had not come this morning with such a tale. I know I must do something about it. I am a beloved woman now, and I should act. But I have not yet even told Little Buck. He should be told. He is headman. Since Four Paws died he has been headman. He should be the first to know, but all day I have kept silent. I have been thinking, remembering.

I need Mink today. So many times I have needed him, but never more than now. It is not easy to be one of the beloved circle. He tried to tell me that. I heard him tell me, but I never thought it would come to me—a woman. It was the fever. So many wise ones died. It was natural that the people would turn to me. They knew Mink had walked with me, that he had told me things. But he did not tell me everything. That is the pity.

So much of our knowledge has been lost. In our town only one priest survived the fever. And he was young. He does not know all the old ones knew. Traveler has been studying with him, learning what he knows. But how much better if Mink could have been his teacher. And how much better if Mink were here now to listen to Traveler's story. Would he, too, say it was an omen?

More than ten years have gone by since the strangers left, more than ten years without a word of them. I want to believe that they have gone forever, that they have returned to their sunless land, and we will never hear of them again.

But now Traveler has come to me with this story. He came this morning and told me that as he stood guard on the palisade last night, he saw Immortals in the cornfield. They rode beasts, he said—perhaps deer, large deer, though he saw no antlers. Two Immortals riding at the head held torches, held them high to show the way across the field. Traveler said that he saw light glinting from their heads and bodies as if they were clothed in metal. He said that as they passed before him there was no sound, not even the sounds of the night. Because of the silence he took it to be a dream. He thought he had been sleeping. But in the first light of dawn he climbed down from the bastion and went out into the cornfield to look. He found a path trampled through the field, the stalks laid flat, or almost so. And there were no tracks to be seen. No tracks of any kind. Nothing at all. Just corn laid flat, trampled by Immortals.

Traveler believes it was an omen. And if it was, there is no question of its meaning. He says we should call a council this very evening.

I myself would like to think it was nothing more than youthful dreaming. I would like to think that the stalks were pulled down by raccoons. Or that a herd of deer ran through, real deer and riderless. Or that perhaps a whirlwind came through in the night, silently as whirlwinds sometimes go, without a sound.

But Traveler is a younger twin. He has the power to see.

AN AFTERWORD

Assuming for a moment that Rain Dove and Traveler were real sixteenth-century Cherokees, the plague through which they suffered in the 1520s was indeed but the first in a long series of tragic events that would befall their people. Of course, Rain Dove and Traveler could not be real, not in a literal sense, for the Cherokees at that time had not yet developed a way of writing their language and therefore could leave us no record of their individual lives. All of the people in this book are fictional, but their character and behavior are consistent with our general knowledge of the Indians of this period, as established by archaeologists, historians, and anthropologists. As for the larger events, these are specifically true and are documented in the European record of the discovery and exploration of America.

Having seen how a Cherokee woman might have experienced these larger events, we may ask how these same events appear in our history books. In changing our viewpoint from Cherokee to European, dates suddenly become important. The chronology of the events in this book begins with the year 1503, eleven years after Columbus' first voyage. For this year historical documents are yet silent about North America, but we know from the research of archaeologists that Cherokee Indians were living at that time among the foothills and mountains of the southern Appalachians.

1503   As in all other years, babies were born in Cherokee villages. One infant, a girl, might have been named Rain Dove, though there is no record of her existence.

1513   Ponce de Leon made the first known Spanish landing on the coast of what is now the United States. It was a brief encounter. The Indians of southern Florida resisted the invasion.

In the next few years, several Spanish expeditions sailed along the Atlantic and Gulf coastlines of southeastern North America, sometimes coming into the mouths of rivers, occasionally venturing ashore.

1519   Smallpox broke out for the first time on the Caribbean island of Hispaniola. It spread rapidly through the Indian population of this and neighboring islands and reached the Central American mainland with the first conquistadors. The death rate among the Indians from smallpox and other European diseases that accompained it—measles, chicken pox, typhus, and influenza, among others—is conservatively estimated at 30 to 50 percent of entire populations.

1521   Two Spanish ships, one under the command of a captain employed by Lucas Vásquez de Ayllón, landed on the Carolina coast. The Indians received the Spaniards as guests. The Spaniards, in return, enticed a large number of their hosts onto their ships and sailed away with them to Hispaniola where the Indians were to be sold as slaves. Among the captives was a man who was later taken to Spain and became known to the Spaniards as Francisco of Chicora.

1525   Planning to found a colony on the Carolina coast, Lucas Vásquez de Ayllón sent his captain back to explore the area and to take from each native province one or two Indians to be trained as interpreters for the colony.

1526   On a balmy summer day Ayllón landed on the Carolina coast with 500 colonists, 89 horses, a number of black slaves, and 3 Dominican friars. Francisco of Chicora had been brought along to serve as an interpreter, but he promptly escaped and returned to his people.

    The colony lasted barely half a year. Two-thirds of the colonists died of disease and starvation. By October, Ayllón himself was dead. In midwinter, after bloody strife between factions in the colony, the Spaniards abandoned their effort and returned to Hispaniola.

1539   Twelve years after the Ayllón colony was abandoned, Hernando de Soto landed on the coast of Florida with an army of more than 600 and began a cruel 4-year journey through the interior of southeastern North America. In time, the army reached the country just inland and upriver from the aborted Ayllón colony. There they saw abandoned Indian towns, empty and overgrown with weeds. Through interpreters, they asked the Indians the reason for it. The Indians explained that there had recently been a plague in the land. Before the plague, the Indians said, the country was very populous.

De Soto's army proceeded on its murderous way, going as far north as the Cherokee country in the southern Appalachians before turning southward again and then westward to the Mississippi River.

These are events which have never been regarded as greatly significant in our history books, and perhaps they never will be. They are but obscure sentences in the first paragraph of the story we tell about ourselves. And the Indians, so momentously affected by these "minor" events, are never glimpsed by us at all.

This book, then, is about a people who lived and died on the other side of history, just beyond our view.

J.R.

About the Author

Joyce Rockwood was born in Ames, Iowa, but she has spent most of her life in Georgia. She studied anthropology at the University of Georgia. She insists on gardening organically; likes country music on the radio; tolerates old dogs; hates to cook; loves to chop firewood. She and her husband, Charles Hudson, also an anthropologist, live near Danielsville, Georgia. Her previous novel about Cherokees, *Long Man's Song*, received wide critical acclaim.